The Old Ways
Volume 2

CURATED BY HOLLEY CORNETTO
EDITED BY S.O. GREEN

EERIE RIVER PUBLISHING

The Old Ways: Volume 2

Eerie River Publishing
www.EerieRiverPublishing.com
Hamilton, Ontario Canada
This book is a work of fiction. Names, characters, places, events,
organizations and incidents are either part of the author's imagination
or are used fictitiously. Any resemblance to actual persons, living or dead,
or actual events is purely coincidental.

Ebook ISBN 978-1-990245-88-6
Paperback ISBN 978-1-990245-90-9

Edited by S.O. Green
Curated by Holley Cornetto
Cover Design Michelle River

ORIGINAL STORIES BY

Elin Olausson
Marisca Pichette
Dixon March
Rob Francis
Kay Hanifen
Derek Heath
Selah Janel
Amanda Casile
Bryson Richard
Michael Quay
Mackenzie Hurlbert
Sarah Day

STORIES

WOODLAND

By Elin Olausson

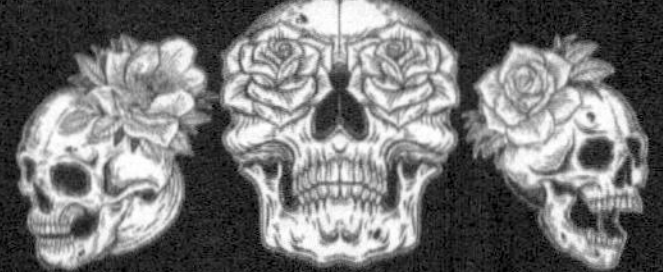

We moved to Liden because of that thing my father had done, because there were houses to rent, because there were no cops or social workers for miles.

"I'm doing this for you guys," my father said, his voice piercing through the noise from the car stereo. The radio hadn't picked up any signal for almost an hour, but he refused to turn it off. "Fresh air, nature, a yard to play in. If you want, we could get us a goat."

Selma and I were much too old for childish games, and we had never expressed any desire to own pets. He hummed some eighties tune, a rock ballad, and Selma leaned to whisper in my ear, "We should have escaped at the gas station."

Her breath smelled of raspberry-flavored gum, and she spoke just a little too loud, as if she was taunting our father, wanting him to hear.

The house was square, a cube of bricks in different shades of brown. Even I could see that the roof needed replacing.

"Well, this isn't so bad." He strode around the yard with his hands in his pockets like he owned the place, like he had the means to buy instead of rent. Selma and I knew he barely had money enough for that. "Look, girls. There's an oak."

The tree was enormous, covering the house in shadow. It looked sick and wilting, and I didn't understand why my father seemed impressed by it.

"I think I'll put up a swing. A tree like that should have a swing, shouldn't it?"

The dusty yard, the fence, the weed-spattered dirt road outside—our new world was as ugly as the old one, but there at least we'd had places to go. Selma aimed a kick at the Toyota but pulled back in time, before he noticed.

"We'll have a fine old time out here, won't we?" He grinned, that cheap Hollywood smile that had fooled Mom. "Selma, Veronika. Got any suggestions for goat names?"

I shrugged; Selma did the same. The evening was hot, and I wanted my phone, wanted a bed to sleep in that I didn't have to share with my sister. Our father kept grinning. I wished that I'd been brave enough to ask what he had to be pleased about.

An approaching car made us turn our heads to the road. It was a red pickup truck, and my father gasped when it passed through our gates, as if he thought whoever drove that car carried a police badge and a gun.

The front door opened and a woman stepped out, tall and sturdy, dressed in dungarees and a baseball cap. Her hair was blonde, or grey depending on the light, the same color as the dust at our feet.

"Welcome to Liden." She eyed each of us in turn. "I'm Eivor, your landlord. You'll have seen my farm on your drive over, I expect."

My father beamed. "Thank you."

He enjoyed meeting new people, slipping into the role he loved the most—charming, friendly single dad. Any second now, he'd mention us and say something cringey about how pretty we were.

"These are my girls, Selma and Veronika. I don't know how I ended up having such beautiful daughters. It's nothing short of a mystery."

Eivor nodded as if he'd made an interesting remark. "I'm thrilled that you are here. Liden is a tiny place, as you've seen already. We rarely get any new residents."

"Oh, we are excited to start our life out here. The girls will thrive."

As if he knew anything about us. Eivor looked at me and I got the feeling that she knew what I was thinking, but then she turned back to my father and the feeling was gone.

"I'll leave you to it. I just wanted to say hello and let you know that you can contact me anytime if you're having trouble. This old place has its quirks, and it might take some getting used to."

"That's most kind of you." He threw his arm over Selma's shoulders and she didn't flinch. He wasn't the only one who could act. "I'm sure we'll be fine though."

Eivor's mouth twitched as if she disagreed, but it was such a tiny movement I might have imagined it.

"Goodnight to you. Like I said, just give me a call if you need anything."

She got back into her car and drove off. We stayed quiet until the pickup truck was out of sight.

"Nice of her to offer," my father said, "but we'll handle things ourselves."

Once he'd located the house key, we went inside with our crammed plastic bags, our school backpacks filled with clothes and cheap jewelry. Selma found a bedroom and I another. We threw ourselves on the beds and coughed when dust whirled up around us.

"I hate this," she said.

"I hate this," I echoed.

We curled up on the windowsill in her room and watched the oak that dominated the yard. Down on the first floor, our father was whistling a mad tune, and Selma scratched at a scab on her knee, tore it off as if it were a band-aid, put it in her mouth.

"You're gross," I said, but she kept chewing, and I didn't mind as much as I should've.

"He'll grow tired of it," she said, when she was done, the scab dissolving in her belly. "A few months, tops, then he'll want to go back home."

I wasn't so sure. "He likes it here," I said. "He thinks we like it too."

Selma leaned back and I caught a whiff of her smell, raspberry gum and green apple shampoo. "I don't think I like it anywhere."

School was out of the question, as were part-time jobs, friends and parties. We repainted the porch because our father made us. We baked bread and his favorite cinnamon cookies. He told us he'd build a chicken coop, or a shed for the bikes we didn't have, but most of the time, he sat on the porch with his eyes on the road. As if the police could never find him as long as he kept watch.

The local store was a forty-minute walk away, and our father declared it our duty to handle grocery shopping.

"If we get to take the car," I said, and he laughed. That soft, melodious laugh that made people like him when they shouldn't.

"You'll have to wait a few more years, sweetheart. Walking is good for you, and once we've settled in, I'll get you girls some bikes. How does that sound?"

So we headed down the road on Friday with our backpacks and the list he'd written, neatly specifying which brands to buy and how many boxes of this and that. It was hot, though it wasn't even nine in the morning, and flies buzzed around our mouths and ears.

When we left the store, backpacks bursting with milk cartons and canned beans, Eivor's red pickup drove by, then stopped. She rolled her window down and called out to us.

"Girls! Need a ride?"

The truck smelled of hay and something else. A herb I couldn't place. Selma told me to get in first, so I did, sitting next to Eivor in the wide front seat.

Her hands on the wheel were tan and wrinkly, and she wore chipped red nail polish that didn't suit her. "Your dad out working?"

"No, he…" Selma's voice trailed off. We'd been taught not to talk about our father with strangers.

"He's just sitting on the porch," I said, and Selma elbowed my arm.

"Oh. Okay." Eivor snorted. "Not that it's any of my business, but it doesn't seem fair. How old are you? Thirteen, fourteen? Here's what we'll do—you come to me when he sends you to the store, and I'll drive you, or one of my farmhands will. I'm not taking no for an answer."

As if we were going to argue with her. When she dropped us off by the roadside some hundred yards from the house, she narrowed her eyes at us and said she was on our side.

"I'm guessing that your dad isn't, so someone has to be."

If he noticed that we returned much earlier than expected, he didn't comment on it. He unpacked the groceries and put each item in place, stacked the milk cartons with the front side up.

"This is what I'm talking about. Collaboration. Working together as a family."

That night, Selma and I sat under the oak and let its dead leaves fall into our hair. She twisted her woven bracelet between her fingers, the one she had made for Mom but had never been able to give her.

"How long do you think it will take?" she said.

I didn't need to ask what she meant. We were as flimsy as

the leaves; we flew in whatever direction he wanted. From the porch, I heard him singing an old song, liqueur sweet.

"Let's just hope for something good," I said, as Mom used to do whenever the coin jar was empty, but unlike her, I knew that nothing good was coming our way.

Eivor's farm was huge, the pastures surrounding it reminding me of prairies and plains, of the Western comics I'd read as a child. There were massive trees growing around the house, oaks and chestnuts and maples. She came out of the barn to greet us, sweat staining her gray shirt. There were some other women around, booted, hair in ponytails or braids. They nodded to us but didn't speak.

"You should come by sometime, if you want work," she told us, when we were in the car. "I could use some extra help this time of year."

Selma stretched out next to me and I thought about our father, glass of milk in his hand, watching the road. "Maybe."

Eivor waited for us while we did our shopping. The old man behind the counter chuckled as he scanned our groceries, weighing each apple in his shriveled hand.

"So, you know Eivor." There was something tinny about his voice, something robotic. "She's been here as long as anyone can remember. She knows how to handle herself."

"Okay." Selma and I rolled our eyes, but he didn't seem to notice. Or maybe he didn't care.

"Don't cross her though. Plenty of people have made that mistake."

When we came back to the car, Eivor glanced toward the store and huffed. "You talked to Allan, didn't you? I'm sure he had a lot to say about me."

"Not really," I lied.

Eivor reached into the plastic bag at my feet and grabbed a tomato, popped it into her mouth. "Allan is harmless, but he blabbers. That doesn't mean you have to listen to what he says."

Our father was out in the yard when we came home. He was angry. I saw it right away, the way he seemed to have turned to stone with his jaw set, his eyes darker than usual.

"That woman," he said. "I'm not a fool, you know. I heard the car."

"She wanted to help."

It didn't work, just like we knew it wouldn't. It was all part of the cycle, the one that began with goats and swings and ended badly. Mom had seen the pattern, but she had seen it much too late.

"You're grounded." He snatched the grocery receipt from my hand, started studying it as he talked. "Go to your rooms right now. Don't come down until I say so."

After that, we sat on the windowsill in Selma's room, watching the garden. The oak. If we opened the window, we could reach the nearest branch, climb down, be free, but of course we didn't because it wouldn't work. When the branches tapped against the window-glass that night, we put the pillows over our heads and went back to sleep.

He let us out the next morning, said he was sorry, offered lemon tea and cake. "Things will be better from now on. Just as long as we stay together."

Eivor came by in the afternoon, jeans grimy and worn. "I've asked the girls to help out at the farm. Unless you've got something against it."

My father gave her the usual grin, but it looked unnatural, as if he'd put on a mask. "The girls are too young for farm work, don't you think? In a couple of years, maybe."

"Maybe." She pursed her lips before easing into a smile that didn't look any more natural than his. "Either way, you should all join the festivities this weekend. It's the Tree Feast.

A local celebration, you probably haven't heard of it…but we're proud of our traditions here in Liden."

"Thank you for the invitation." My father beamed as if he'd been handed an award. "We'll try to make it."

"Oh, don't worry." Eivor glanced at Selma and me. "We'll come and get you."

He was fuming after she left, spitting into the dirt. "She needs to mind her own business. And you two had better stay away from her."

We nodded, poured him milk, made lasagna for dinner. Selma whispered about calling the police and I inhaled her raspberry scent, pretending not to hear.

The Tree Feast. We watched the oak, heard its branches tap against the window. We talked about Mom and about that thing our father had done, while he sang downstairs in a voice that grew louder and hoarser with every day.

"He won't let us go," Selma said. "Eivor can't do anything about that."

I knew it was true and yet I refused to believe it, just like that time when Mom died. "Maybe she'll find a way to persuade him."

Selma snorted. "She's not young and pretty, in case you hadn't noticed."

The leaves fell outside, heaped up around the tree trunk. It was far too early, a month left until autumn. As a child, I had loved playing among fallen leaves, using them as hideaways, but now the sight made me sad and I turned my eyes away.

"What do you think the Tree Feast is like?" I asked.

Selma leaned her forehead against the window-glass, and

her long hair hid her face. "Like midsummer but less fun. I don't know. And it doesn't matter because we won't be going."

I thought about leaves, hollow trunks and hiding places. Downstairs, my father started howling.

Eivor came by the next morning. We heard the roaring of her truck, the footsteps, the knock on the door.

"Girls!" our father called. "Come down, will you?"

As if he wanted an audience to the scene that was about to begin the moment he opened the door. When we came into the hallway, Eivor was there, arms crossed, while he talked and gestured.

"Always a pleasant surprise to have a visit from a neighbor," he said, his voice much too loud. "How's life on the farm? Busy days, I bet."

"Yes." Eivor glanced over at me and my sister. "That's why I came over. Two of my girls have called in sick, they won't be back for a week. Flu, most likely."

"It can be rough, the flu," our father interrupted. "I had a bad case of it once, thought I'd never make it."

"Anyway, I came to ask if your daughters would be interested in helping out this week. I know what you said last time, but it would only be a few hours a day and they'd get paid, of course."

Please, Dad—the words were on my tongue, sticky sour like that lemon candy Selma had loved when we were kids. But I had stopped calling him Dad many years ago and I wouldn't start now.

"Selma. Veronika." He didn't look at us, just motioned for us to come over. "Did you tell Eivor that you needed work? Did you tell her that I don't provide for you?"

"Don't know," I said, because I honestly could not remember.

"I think there's been a misunderstanding." Eivor took a step back out on the porch. "I must have gotten it wrong, I'm sorry."

"We all make mistakes." My father put his hand over his chest in a ridiculous gesture that would have made me laugh if I wasn't afraid of him. "Have a lovely day now."

Eivor gave me a look before leaving, heading back to her truck. My father spun around. He was grinning, and something about that grin made me wish I wasn't standing so close to him.

"You'll regret it if you ever talk to that woman again." He put his hand on my shoulder and squeezed. "Now go back upstairs."

We didn't speak until we were in Selma's room with the door shut.

"She's trying to help us," I said, watching as yet another oak-leaf fell.

"I don't think she's a good person," Selma replied, and I thought, *She could still help us.*

The weekend came. Our father had brought alcohol home from God-knows-where, beer and red wine, heavy bottles of vodka. Had he gone into town while we were sleeping? We tiptoed around him like trained mice, cooked dinner, swept the porch free of dust.

"You do as you're told, that's how I like it." He chuckled, lifted the bottle to his lips. "Your mother could have learnt a thing or two if she'd been around."

This was the lowest point, rock bottom. I wished the cycle would speed up so we'd get back to the beginning, even though I hated that too because his good mood was never real. In the evening, after doing the dishes, Selma and I hid in her room and whispered about Mom. I sobbed, so did she, and that's why we didn't hear the cars at first. Not until they were already in the yard, engines roaring, laughter rising to the sky. Chanting.

"Out! Out! Out! Out!"

We pressed our faces to the window. The yard was filled with people holding torches, people with wreaths in their long hair. Women, all of them women.

The door burst open just as we came down the stairs. Eivor, dressed strangely in what looked like a long, white nightgown. Her hair reached almost down to her waist, and she gave us a smile.

"It's time."

Selma grabbed my arm as chanting women filled the hallway, following Eivor inside the house. I recognized one or two from the farm, but they looked different now. Their eyes shone and Selma breathed raspberry-whispers into my ear. *Drugged. Psychotic. Crazy.* They disappeared into the living room and over their monotonous chanting I heard screams, cursing.

"What the hell are you doing? I'm calling the police!"

He was tied up, dragged along by Eivor and a large, red-haired woman. He aimed kicks at them, but they were fast and he was so drunk he could barely stand.

"Come along," Eivor told me and Selma, so we did. I still don't know if it was because we wanted to, or because we were afraid of what would happen if we refused.

They dropped him belly-down on the bed of the truck as if he were a heavy bag, a piece of cargo. The truck bed was all grimy, smeared with oil, and when he twisted his face to the side it was covered in dirt.

"Girls, you have to do something." There was something

strange about his voice, a thickness, as if his throat had clogged up. "Stop this."

Some of the women came up to us with wreaths, put them on our heads. The flowers had a heavy smell that I didn't like at first, but after a while, I forgot it was there.

"The poor old oak," Eivor said, lifting her arms toward the tree. "It's dying. It needs a rebirth."

The women around us started smiling. "Rebirth, rebirth, rebirth."

"You're insane!" my father cried, but the filth on his face made him hard to recognize and I could trick myself into believing that he was just an unfortunate stranger.

"We should begin." Eivor looked directly at Selma and me. "Bring the gift of life, make the world beautiful. Take away the sadness. *Kvinnor, sjung*!"

The chanting grew louder as she crossed the yard, walked toward the truck. He wailed like a baby, but I didn't feel sorry, because Mom had sounded worse and it hadn't made him stop. Eivor opened the passenger door and took out something shiny. An axe.

"You might want to look away," she told us, but we didn't.

Her white gown was dripping with blood when she had brought the blade down five times. After twenty, her face was a gleaming red mask that made me think of Halloween and the costume my father had worn once, the leather clinging to his skull.

The women carried the pieces to the oak, singing solemnly as they buried them in a hole in the trunk. Blood colored the dust, made it shimmer. Eivor came last, carrying the heart and the head.

"Accept our offering, Father Oak, and come back to life."

Afterwards, when the other women had left, she came up to us and smiled. She was still soaked in his blood, his fluids, but the crazed shine in her eyes was gone.

"I know what he did to your mother. We get men like that

out here sometimes. That's why we have the Tree Feast."

"And if there isn't a bad man around when a tree is dying?" I asked. She narrowed her eyes, as if she was intrigued by the question, but she didn't answer.

"Stay in the house," she said instead. "Come work for me. We love new people here in Liden. In a way, we're all one big family."

"Okay," I said, or maybe it was Selma.

Eivor left and we sat on the porch, wreaths wilting, the air around us metallic. We slept in the same bed that night, dreamt identical nightmares about that hole in the oak and what it hid.

When we woke, the birds were chirping. I went to the window to pull the curtains aside, then called for Selma to come see.

The oak was vibrant with color. Each leaf was spring-green, and the branches reached toward the sky.

"The leaves aren't falling anymore," Selma said, fingers tight around the windowsill.

We headed outside, still in our pajamas, gravel stinging our feet. The air was fresh and there were no blood specks in the dirt, no traces of what had happened last night. The hole in the oak scared us but we had to look, so we did.

There was nothing. No hole at all, just a healthy tree trunk that felt sun-warm and rough against my fingers.

A rich foliage over our heads, a yard to run across, a house to live in.

When we went to Eivor's farm to work the next day, she didn't mention the Tree Feast, and neither did we. We sat in the shade of her mighty trees, the oaks and chestnuts and maples, and we drank lemonade and thought about the house that was ours.

And the tree that would always watch over us.

SPINES

By Marisca Pichette

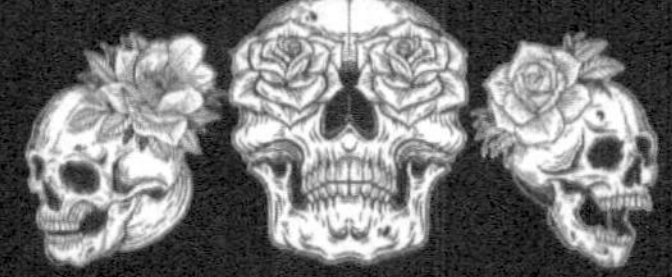

The trees watch. The trees sustain.

Magda groaned. Already, her joints prickled in response to the damp air, and as she opened her eyes, she saw that more shadows than sunlight dappled the floor of her cottage. She cursed quietly as she pushed the heavy quilts back, exposing her arms to the chill morning air.

Today would not be a good day. She could feel it in her aging bones.

Though she wore thick wool socks she'd knitted herself, the floor still made its temperature known as she stood, tugging her shawl up onto her shoulders.

Magda made her way to the kitchen and groaned again at the ashes in the fireplace. A few preliminary pokes confirmed her suspicions. The fire was thoroughly dead. She leaned the poker against the brick and went to the front door.

A slight drizzle deepened the shadows between the bushes outside. On the other side of their hunched, green bodies, Magda could see the trees.

Their pale forms stretched into the sky, branching from thick trunks to spindly arms cut out against the clouds. They had mostly lost their leaves, but a few membranous shapes clung like bats to the higher branches. These, too, were pale, vitality leeched out of them by the cold.

Magda sighed, breath fogging the glass. She would hardly fill half a bucket with the trees that color. She braced herself and stepped outside under the porch. Autumn was coming to an end and the damp was worsening. It wouldn't be long before Magda had snow to contend with, on top of everything else.

She gathered a few bundles of straw from her supply and tucked them under her arm. With her free hand, she scooped up some coal, enough to last an hour or two and cook her breakfast.

When she was back inside, Magda coaxed a fire to life and hung her teapot over the fresh flames. She was soon sitting at her table, cup in hand, cracking open an egg with a spoon. That was when someone knocked on her door.

She paused, her spoon mid-tap. By the tempo of the knock, it was someone shy. She waited for them to knock two more times, then got to her feet and opened the door.

Frila was standing under Magda's porch. Her skin was almost as pale as the distant trees.

"Magda," Frila said, bobbing her head like a hen. "May I come in?"

Magda squinted at the young woman. She didn't appreciate early calls. "What is it you need?"

"Froth and I were hoping... Well, you know we've been married three months now. I was hoping to..." She trailed off, eyes staring, too big for her bony face.

"You want a child," Magda said.

Frila smiled, bobbing her head again. "Yes."

"When?"

The girl stared at her. Magda thought about her tea, getting cold on the table. She asked again, "When do you want the child? Are you ready for it?"

"Yes! We have a cot, and blankets, and toys—"

"And food? You'll be able to feed it?"

Magda didn't trust the girl's thinness. Froth, she recalled, was likewise lean.

Frila nodded, smiling with near-colorless lips. Magda was torn between inviting her in and spoiling her breakfast, or continuing to cool her house while she stood here with the door open, waiting for the girl to get to the point.

She could feel her shoulder growing stiff from holding the door. "Well, if you're sure you're ready, I can arrange to form the child today," she said. "Will you be home with your husband at four o'clock?"

Frila beamed. She bobbed several times. "Yes, yes! Thank you, Magda!"

The girl hurried away. Magda closed her door and returned to a cup of tepid tea and an egg with broken shards of shell stuck to the white. She sat, chewing on her tongue. Perhaps if everyone in Branch chose to have their babies in the fall, she wouldn't have to trudge out to the trees in the winter.

Magda ate her egg and added hot water to her tea. Then, she put the damper down on her fire, pulled a wool dress over her shift and struggled into her coat. She paused at the door to slide her feet into boots and hands into gloves sewn from leathern leaves the trees had dropped the autumn before. Last, she stooped to pick up her tools—a pail, a hammer and a metal spout.

She opened the door and went out to tap the trees.

There were six of them, arranged in a circle shadowed by interlacing vines, the tallest plants that could even begin to challenge the height and girth of the trees. As Magda approached, her hammer and spout rattling in her pail, she could see that she'd been right. The trees were not only unusually pale; their skins were riddled with goosebumps, protesting the chill air. She would be lucky to get a third of a pail.

She entered the ring and set down her tools, flexing her wrinkled hands within their thick gloves. She was the only tree tender in Branch. That wasn't to say she was the only one who knew how to tap the trees and not get herself killed in the process. Plenty of others had seen her at work. They could have tapped the trees themselves, if they desired.

But if anyone but the tree tender so much as scratched a tree, they were condemned to blooding.

Magda had seen enough in her life, and watching a human get staked in the middle of the trees and emptied of their blood was not a sight she cared to witness. She heard the screams from her cottage, along with murmurs and shouts from the crowd that stood witness.

If one died naturally, one's body was buried outside of the trees, flesh and blood returned to the sustaining soil. A blooding was unique, forceful. Remove the blood before its time, cut short the trees' lease of it. What remained of the corpse was then buried outside the bounds of Branch, with the exception of the spine. That was burned.

Stealing from the trees severed one's right to one day be part of them.

Magda turned to the first tree. Its trunk was wider than her hips, and it rose high above her head, branching out like some multi-armed beast. Each branch terminated in a bunch of twigs that resembled fingers, jointed and pulsing with veins.

Though most of the leaves had fallen, Magda could still see a few clinging to the branches, semi-transparent membranes like bat wings. They matched her gloves and boots, both made from the material—the strongest leather in Branch.

She turned her attention back to the tree's trunk. Its pale skin was riddled with scars from where she'd tapped it before. She circled the tree until she found an unblemished patch and positioned her pail against the trunk. Raising her spout and hammer, she tapped the tree.

The sharp edge of the spout cut easily through the layers of skin. Almost immediately, a trickle of blood issued forth, pattering against the bottom of the pail. As Magda held the spout steady, the trickle slowed to no more than an irritatingly inconsistent drip-dripping.

After a few minutes, she ripped out the spout. It wasn't worth waiting any longer. Today was not a good day for tapping.

But Frila and Froth wanted a child.

Magda worked her way from one tree to the next, circling the grove until she'd managed to fill just over a third of the pail with blood. The resulting gashes in the trees wept red in the damp air. They would heal overnight, adding new scars to the trunks.

Magda trudged back to her cottage, careful not to spill a drop from her pail. Blood from the trees was more than a substance with the power to create life, to create a child.

It was also deadly.

Frila and Froth would doubtless want to watch her form their child from the blood, but being in the same room as a forming was itself a dangerous choice. Magda covered as much of her skin as she could and stood far back once the shape was made. Children tended to squirm, and drops could fly all the way to the walls if the child was spirited. Looking at Frila and Froth, Magda doubted that would be the case. Besides, the sad quantity of blood promised a small, if not sickly, child.

Suited to its parents, Magda thought, as she let herself back into the warm interior of her home and set the pail by the door. She pulled the gloves from her hands and glanced at the clock. She still had several hours until she was expected. Plenty of time for the blood to warm, and for her to relax.

Magda spent the hours before the birth reading, working on a fresh shawl, and darning a pair of socks. Her cottage was quiet. Too quiet. Whenever she stopped working, she remembered the voices that used to fill it—a succession of lovers over the years, warming her bed and making mistakes.

They always made mistakes. Small ones at first, culminating in the final mistake, which took their life.

There can only be one tender of the trees, Magda had

heard, again and again. It took her many partners to realize what this truly meant. She could not have lovers. Not forever. The trees took them, one by one.

The memories twisted through the cottage, refusing to drain away with her dying fire. Come four o'clock, Magda put on her thickest dress and left, making her way into Branch.

Technically, her cottage was part of the village, but the closest Magda had to human company were the pails of blood she carried. The center of Branch lay a half-hour's walk to the south, and Magda's shoulder ached from carrying by the time she knocked on Frila and Froth's door.

It was the husband who answered. Pale as his wife, with drooping blue eyes and a crooked nose. Magda thought he looked a little like a man she'd at one time loved, before he attempted to tap one of the trees while she was sleeping. She'd found him the next morning, a heap of empty, glistening skin.

The trees took everyone from her, eventually.

Do not touch the blood.

Of course, they insisted on being present for the forming. With Froth and Frila watching from the next room, Magda covered her body with leather, leaving only her eyes bare, to see her work.

She picked up the pail and poured the blood out onto the floor of their cottage. The puddle spread, dark and shining. She'd warmed it by the fire, but it had coagulated on the walk to Branch. The resulting consistency was almost perfect for forming. With a long-handled brush, Magda coaxed the blood into the shape of a child.

She was the only midwife in Branch. Any child that was desired, she painted on the floor of the house that would become its home.

She drew legs and a face. She pulled the blood into hands and soft buttocks. She did not determine a sex—that was for the blood to decide.

The last detail she added was the spine, drawn in sharp strokes down the middle of the painting. Around this, the child would form.

When the image was complete, Magda set the bloodstained brush back in her pail. She stepped back, almost as far as Frila and Froth, and waited.

While she'd painted, the blood had begun to seep into the floorboards. Now, it shifted, coalescing.

At first, the image was only churning blood, a red-black swirl on the stained floor. Then, a grinding sound announced the development of bones, and Magda saw them: maggot-white lumps in the flowing blood. They snapped together, forming the spine, before the rest of the skeleton spooled out, snapping into place. Ribbons of fine muscle wrapped over the bones, speckled with flecks of cartilage. Pale, bulbous organs notched together, before a ripple of skin wrapped around everything and flopped onto the floor in the middle of what remained of the blood.

Here was the dangerous part. Magda held her breath as the infant squirmed into shape, legs extending out from a ball of flesh that almost halved to create a head. Arms formed from blunt nubs of skin into latticed hands with infantile nails.

The face was always the last to emerge.

Flesh split and blood poured back onto the floor as eyes, mouth, nose and ears were torn into existence. And with the final, untethered muscle—the tongue—the child of Frila and Froth cried.

With this wail, what blood remained beaded up on the floor and rolled towards the infant, crawling up over its fleshy legs and arms and disappearing back into the mouth. All the while, it thrashed, screaming for parents it didn't know.

Frila tried to run to the child, but Magda snatched her arm, holding her back.

"Wait. It isn't safe yet."

Frila stared at her son—Magda could see the limp lump of flesh between its legs that marked it as a boy—until the last of the blood was pulled back into the child.

Now it is done.

Magda released Frila and the girl hurried across the room. She picked up the child, holding him close. Goosebumps covered his tiny body, like the trees of his making.

Walking back to her cottage, the empty pail swinging in her grasp, Magda imagined her fire, dead in the grate. She pictured the dark rooms that awaited her, the cold that would continue to worsen. Her heels felt bruised, her knees strained from crouching to paint.

As she drew close to her home, she looked out at the trees standing pale in the dark.

Without them, Branch would die out, gradually, as no new children were formed. The trees sustained the village. Without their blood—and Magda's painting—no more births would take place. Branch would wither and die like leaves in winter.

The trees stood for life, for the future. But standing in the dark, Magda remembered Gret's birth—that was the name Frila and Froth gave to the child—and all the births that had come before that. She had seen too many times how humans were made, and unmade.

She looked from the tress to her empty cottage. Over the years, how many partners had she enticed into her bed, leading them into a life that wouldn't last? She hadn't known what would happen. Not at first. After the first three, she'd suspected. But she'd hoped.

And her hoping had killed them. Her hope made the trees laugh, luring her lovers again and again into their circle to die in a heap of empty, bleeding skin.

Each she discovered the next morning, dread mounting as she woke to a cold space behind her, missing shoes and coat, and the distant, pale shapes of the trees.

Magda told no one of how her lovers died. Instead, she buried them within the circle, against the laws of Branch. Against the laws of the trees she served.

The trees that controlled her existence and denied her everything.

As she looked at the distant grove with its six pallid trunks, their canopies spread out like fingers gripping the sky, she decided to end the cycle.

Never kill a tree. Kill a tree, and you kill a child. A hundred children.

Magda set down her pail under the porch. She picked up the ax that leaned against the side of her cottage. She walked towards the trees.

The night was silent, pregnant. As winter took hold, squeezing the warmth away, the trees would stop bleeding. For five months, Magda would be unable to get more than a drop of blood from any of the six trunks on her doorstep.

No blood, no pay. From today's forming, she'd earned six loaves of bread and a dozen fertilized eggs. Froth would deliver them in the morning, ensuring Magda had food for the weeks to come, and at least a few more chickens to supply her eggs for breakfast.

But how many more births would there be before winter? How much more bread?

Magda was tired. Cold, bruised, and tired. All she would have for company during those long, dark months would be the trees, their pale bodies pinched with goosebumps in a field of snow, covering all that remained of her life beyond.

Magda carried the ax at her side, its head swishing through the grass. She entered the grove.

The trees surrounded her, silent figures in the night. Six ghostly bodies, waiting. Growing. She set the ax down between her feet and worked her cold hands into her gloves. She wrapped her scarf around her nose and mouth and pulled up her hood.

In the center of the grove, there was a stump, an iron rod buried close to its center. This was where the bloodings were carried out, over the carcass of a dead tree. Magda approached it, staring down at the withered, purple flesh, the discolored bone at the center. The tree had a spine running through it like a human. Like a snake.

Many things had spines.

Who killed this one? Magda wondered.

She picked up her ax and walked to the nearest living tree, close enough that she could see the scars adorning its trunk, scars from the tapping she'd done over the long years. Scars from the tenders who came before her.

Will anyone come after?

Magda felt along the tree with one gloved hand. There was a long scar towards the base; it looked like someone had tried to cut down this tree before. They had likely spilled blood onto their skin and ended up like her once-loves, a mound of skin with nothing left to give it shape, give it flair.

After tending the trees for decades, Magda knew how to protect herself. She lined her ax up with the scar.

In the morning, Froth walked up from the village, carrying a basket of bread and eggs. The air was thick with autumn mist, and he was almost on top of the cottage before it revealed itself.

No smoke issued from Magda's chimney. Froth knocked on the door but got no response. After a few more attempts, he found the door to be unlocked and let himself inside.

The fire was dead in the grate. Froth looked around, not moving from the mat on the other side of the door.

"Magda?" he called.

No answer.

Froth set the basket on the floor and closed the door, heading down the path to the grove. He did not plan to enter the ring of trees—that was for the tender only—but he assumed he would be able to see the old woman tapping them from outside.

But, as he made his way through the mist, thinking he should have arrived at the grove by now, his foot sank into a puddle. He looked down and saw it was not water, but blood.

Next to his boot was the stump of a tree. Its body lay in the grass, almost concealed by the tangled strands. Froth stared, bile surging up his throat. He looked further ahead and saw another stump, half-consumed by the mist.

Horror gripped him. He walked forward, dodging further puddles of cold, coagulating blood. A third stump, a fourth.

When he reached the center of what had once been a grove, he saw the last two trees. One was fallen, attached to its base only by a strip of torn and weeping flesh. The sixth tree was cut halfway through, mangled skin bleeding freely onto the wet ground, its spine pale and exposed.

Magda—or the pile of empty skin of whoever did this— was nowhere in sight.

Froth bent over, nausea swarming up his throat. He needed to get back to Branch proper, raise the alarm and...

Do what?

The trees...

Would the last survive? He forced himself to look back at the sixth tree, scarred, pale, and bleeding. With so much cut away, would it make it through the winter?

Froth walked back to Magda's cottage, face clammy with mist and cold. Perhaps the old woman escaped whoever killed the trees. She would know how to save the sixth. He tried to focus on that hope as he opened the door to Magda's cottage and stared inside.

His gaze settled on the floor, seeing something he'd missed before. Bloody footprints, dried brown. Froth swallowed against his fresh nausea. The prints led away from the door, further into the cottage.

He followed them through the house to the bedroom. A pair of boots were tucked neatly by the base of the bed. They were covered in blood. Froth recognized them from the previous day. They'd been inside his house.

Froth raised his gaze to the many quilts that covered the bed. They did not rise and fall, but rested over a motionless lump.

Magda was lying in bed, eyes closed, body cold and still as the air that filled the cottage. On her face lingered a faint, stiff smile.

On the pillow next to her rested an ax.

BUTTERBONE

BY DIXON MARCH

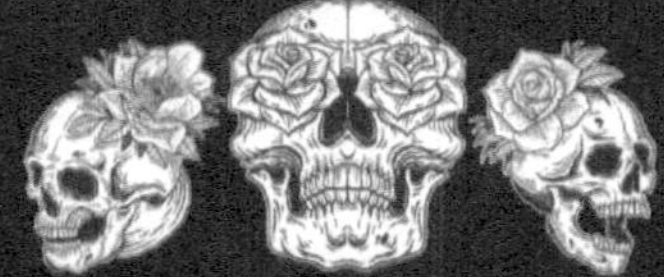

Dano said he didn't eat meat since he started seeing this vegetarian, and now he was 'ovo lacto', which sounded like some spooky shit to Mayson, some incantation like *ovolacto-nickto-verata*, a chant to summon the dead.

Mayson loaded the trunk of the Cadillac with the black plastic package and told himself, not the right time to summon anything. He ruminated on how little he wanted to be here, out in the country with a corpse in the trunk and a psycho white kid behind the wheel. A kid who didn't eat meat. Once this job was over, Mayson was done, retired, forever and ever amen. His employers were none too pleased about it, but they were sensible gangsters. Surely, his old bosses would rather Mayson sit on a beach in Tijuana and nurse a fine drinking habit than risk him talking to the Feds about what he'd been doing for the last twenty years.

Surely, he thought.

From the Cadillac's front seat, Dano hollered a shapeless word, and Mayson took it as a sign it was time to go. Too much purple drank had made Dano a little off. The kid peered at him through the windshield, and the dashboard lights painted him as green as a Florida lawn. The tattoos in the corner of his eyes and on his forehead were inscrutable hieroglyphs. Word was, Dano was on the outs after he shot up a competitor's warehouse in D-town. Bit of a trigger fetish. If they ran into a single cop—any yokel county sheriff out here in the boons—Dano would likely pull some blaze of glory shit with that piece he had under the seat, a Colt Gold Cup in nickel finish, engraved with naked women who were likely not vegetarians.

At the idea of Dano going commando, Mayson's ulcer flared up, a miniature sun in his gut. It would be a rough night regardless, but if he played it smart, he might make it. Once this was over, he could take the Cadillac and drive forever, get lost in the starlight and never have to mop up anyone's bullshit again.

When Mayson opened the passenger side door, Dano grinned at him with untended teeth. "You ever had chick'n?"

"Chicken, yeah." Mayson settled his big body into the coupe and his knees scrunched up to his chest. "You mean chicken?"

"Nah, chick-nnnn. It's like fake meat, made of soy or wheat or someshit. Chews like I dunno, Elmer's glue. You ever eat Elmer's glue?"

"Nah, man. 'fraid not."

"Not even in grade school?" Dano hissed gently between his silver teeth and started the car. "Shit."

Night had fallen, so the lights of the city in the distance blinked on, flashed yellow and white like a field of stars knocked down to earth. Mayson saw his face in the glass of the window and thought he looked ghostly. Fat. He wondered if a diet of ovolactochik'n would help in that area. At his age, likely not. Forty didn't do anyone nice, 'less they were rich fucks with treadmills in their living rooms and personal chefs twirping about the kitchen. He half-expected to be put to pasture any night now.

Forty hit harder, Mayson told himself, to people in his line of work.

Dano put the sedan in gear and sped off past the gravel pits, inched towards sixty-five. Mayson glared at him, wondered how a person in his line of work got to babysitting like this.

"Slow down. We've got cargo."

"Yeah, yeah. I know." Dano eased off. "Who's the guy we're taking it to again? It's a long drive out to nowhere. You said he's a vegetarian too, yeah?"

Mayson glowered at himself in the dark. "They call him the Vegan."

Dano chewed on that a moment, his thoughts in a purple-drank-battered spin behind his eyes.

Then the kid said, "You know, I'm fucking this vegetarian."

Mayson said, "Oh really," and then let Dano tell him about it all over again.

Without the belligerence of the city lights to wash out the sky, the stars came out in a thick rash of glitter. It was dark enough out here that Mayson could see the Milky Way, foggy and strange, and he didn't much care for the sight. The world seemed alien, like they'd taken the wrong road and stumbled onto another planet that only pretended to be earth. He scanned the low, black fields and the patches of sickly trees, and when he found the turn off, he was almost surprised it was there at all.

"Take a left here."

Dano virtually spun the wheel, and the sedan tilted in a sick angle for a moment or two. When the tires fishtailed on the gravel, the contents of the trunk thumped about.

Mayson sucked his teeth and braced a big hand on the ohshit handle. "Nice death wish you got there."

The kid's grill flashed green in the dashboard glow. "I like to live fast."

"Is that why you shot up that shipping office?"

Silence fell in the dark of the cabin like a body dropped from a roof. For a moment, Mayson worried he'd pushed the kid too far. Dano's tattooed hands tightened on the wheel, worried the leather.

Then Dano laughed softly. "That was a misunderstanding, a'ight? Jesus, loose lips out here with you rednecks."

Mayson didn't confront him on the insult. Everyone considered this side of the river bumpkin-ville, including himself at times. He'd grown up in LA. "It's a good night to drive like you want to live, all I'm sayin. Considering our cargo."

"Yeah, who's the meatbag, anyway?" Dano chewed a hangnail off his index finger and spat it aggressively onto the floor. "Gotta admit, after D-town I figured I'd end up in a trunk wrapped in black plastic."

"If I knew who it was, I wouldn't say. Professional courtesy."

"Did you do the one-eight-seven?"

"No." Mayson's reflection in the window appeared narrower, like he'd wasted away the farther they got into the dark countryside. "Did you?"

"Hah, fuck no. They took my AK."

Mayson didn't care for that news. His employers' goal surely was to keep the kid quiet, relaxed out in the country, but restrictions could suggest something more sinister. He checked the road and noted how far out in the boons they were. Pitted gravel road. On every side, grass grew tall and wild. It reminded him of a documentary he'd seen in lockup, about this endangered species of tiger that loved to skulk about the grass and stalk its prey. The grass here looked just like this scene where a slab of meat waited in a clearing and the tiger sprang out on top of it, all claws and black-eyed death.

The road came to a T. Dano braked, and the sedan did that thing new cars did and cut the engine to save gas. The silence overwhelmed the night. Mayson hated it. There was nothing to be heard, not even a stray cricket, and it made his ulcer burn.

Dano asked which way, and Mayson studied the landscape. At the truncated crossroads sat an old street sign, crooked and gray. The words on it had been burned black into the wood. Butterbean Road. Around the sign lay an overgrown field with stalks as tall as a man, leafy and strange, some odd crop of corn gone untended. On every stalk, bulbs at the tip bulged out in a spray of silk, stringy and obscene in a way Mayson couldn't put a name to.

He told Dano, "Go left."

Dano hit the gas pedal. "You been here before?"

"I was given directions."

He did not mention he was told to memorize them, rather than function off any written evidence, paper or digital. He hoped he'd remembered it right. The ol' brain pan leaked from time to time. Too many clocks punched. Most often, these errands were handled by the cleaner anyway, so it wasn't his usual gig. On most occasions, such things fell outside his knee-breaking jurisdiction.

None of this he mentioned to Dano. The kid was likely hazardous when spooked. "It's a mile or two down this road." Mayson hoped he was right.

Farther down the stalks about, the road grew taller, and the sedan lurched about over deep potholes. The stars glittered in their skirt of milk and did nothing to dispel his unease. Earlier, he'd caught sight of the Big Dipper, but now it was gone and the stars' arrangement was unfamiliar. They drove for longer than necessary based on the directions. Even Dano, in his breezy, tough kid act, grew quiet the deeper in they went.

Dano leaned over the wheel to squint through the windshield at the road. "Shoulda hit there by now."

In the dashboard glow, his reflection hovered above the stalks like some disembodied god-alien that Mayson remembered from some show. *Star Trek* or *Flash Gordon* or

Dr. Who, one of those days spent home from school to nurse whatever bang or bruise or broken arm his old man had given him. He stared at Dano's reflection, wide and grim and bald as a space egg.

As they drove, the road narrowed on either side, cluttered with mounds and potholes that did a number on the tires. The stalks grew taller. It seemed like the road vanished beneath them, and Dano swore and hit the brakes. The sedan halted silently, not a squeak. Came to a full stop.

The engine cut out. Dead silence. The glow of the headlights cast the stalks in sharp blue relief. The shadows between them deepened.

"What are you doing?" Mayson glared.

The kid breathed hard. "Home, can't you tell when you've been set the fuck up?"

"What? Don't be stupid."

"You never been cow-tipping." A sad shake of his head.

"The fuck is that?" Mayson's stomach clenched. The car sat dead between the rows of stalks, whatever they were, corn or beans or whatever. He had a sense they were neither, but he would not allow himself to think on it for long. "I don't know anything about cows. I grew up in the city."

"Yeah, well." Dano's shoulders slumped. "I didn't."

Mayson huffed. Us rednecks, indeed. "What's cow-tipping?"

Dano regarded the plants crowded up around the sedan. He spoke dreamily. "They say, *hey, come on out here, we'll have some fun,* and say they're gonna knock over cows, because cows sleep upright, or something, yeah? But then that's just a fucking thing people say, like a myth or something. Because cows don't fucking sleep standing up. You just follow them out in the middle of the night, all the way outta town, and there's this field where nothing's happening and you're like, *is there a bull or some shit?* And they're like, *nah, nah, just stand here, just wait here and I'll go find the cows.*"

If Mayson didn't think it impossible, he'd have thought a little moisture appeared at the rim of Dano's eyes.

The kid kept on. "...and you're standing in this black field in the middle of fuckall knows where, and the moon ain't even out. Just trees and grass, all dark and crawling with shit and you think, the *minute* you think, *there's no fucking cows out here*, that's when you hear the engine start up, whatever junk chevy they drove you out here in, because of course they didn't let you take your own ride, no, because that was never the point, was it?" He gulped air. "The point was to take your ass out into the middle of nowhere and leave you there. You think you'll make it back, but you don't."

Mayson chewed on this for a moment in silence. Dread crawled up his spine. On all sides, the night pressed in. The crop was so tall Mayson could no longer see the stars.

He muttered. "I'm sure the place is just a bit up the road."

Dano panted. Might have been hyperventilating.

Mayson kept an easy tone. "You and me, we'll take care of it, yeah?"

"You do anything bad lately?"

He shrugged. "Our employers are not too thrilled with me right now."

Dano whimpered. "This ain't a job, man. They're getting rid of us."

Mayson nodded softly. He didn't argue. "Either way, we'll take care of it. Do the thing and get the fuck out, because we're fucking professionals. Sound good, killer?"

It took some time, but Dano nodded. He touched the gas pedal gingerly, and the sedan's engine kicked on, emitted a low rumble that helped chase away that godawful silence. The vehicle tumbled on through the jungle of crops.

Mayson did not look into the shadows between the rows too deeply. In that dark was a flutter of deeper shades, movement in an intense, umbral color beyond simple night. It wasn't black but a sense of absence, lightlessness like the bottom of the sea.

He did not mention, not with Dano so riled up, that he sensed something watching them from the deep.

Five or so minutes later, they came upon a battered airstream trailer at the end of the road. Not the type hipsters liked, but a ruin. Collapsed on one end, jagged holes throughout its steel siding, tires deflated in shredded rubber. The weeds around it appeared gnarly and snake-ridden. Beside it sat a gutted old tractor, a rusted body with no bones of an engine.

Around both tractor and trailer circled the strange crop. Out here, the bulbs seemed larger—huge coconut-sized sacs, dark and veiny. Their silk littered the drive.

The sedan pulled up as far as it could go. Dano peered low out the windshield, his shoulders scrunched and ferret-like, his eyes small, blue beads. A twitchy gaze, Mayson noted, and he shook his head at what he was about to do.

"Stay here." Mayson opened his door. "Pop the trunk."

He stepped out, and under his feet, the gravel crunched with an unwholesome noise that reminded him of the sound of chicken bones crunched between the teeth of a feral alley cat.

Mayson watched the trunk lid float up as if touched by spectral hands, and from there he lifted the underfloor to examine again the cargo. Black plastic bags, duct-taped aggressively. Something about the weight was still off and had been the whole time. He put his hands on it, worked it over like a blind man. From inside, something sharp and heavy pricked him. Not quite a bone but a hoof.

He pulled out his boot knife, a Buck 616 styled like a tantō, and worried a small hole into the plastic. Studied the flesh there underneath. Smelled a faint hint of copper and porkfat.

The guy who did the 187, as Dano might say, was a real butcher.

"Is that my delivery?"

The voice startled him. Mayson turned to see a man, an old, white asshole in denim coveralls over a bare chest of sinew and gristle, mean-faced. His head was as round as the bulbs in the stalks. On his scalp was a silky spray of hair in patches. He was toothless and fitted for a soundtrack of banjos, bare-footed with toenails long and curled yellow and matted with soil.

Mayson glowered quietly. "It's a no-contact delivery."

"Mmmm." The Vegan smiled a septic grin. "Would you be so kind as to bring it out back for me?"

Boot knife still palmed, Mayson reached one arm around the cargo and hoisted it over his shoulder, this rack of meat that, for the first time, he was disappointed wasn't human. Any regular dickhead's corpse would have weighed at least fifty more pounds. He was royally screwed, so he might as well see what shit show lay at the end of this road.

"Lead the fucking way," he muttered.

When he passed the sedan, he caught a flash of Dano's face. Eyes wide. He slowly mouthed two words that looked like *cow, tipping*. A puff of his panicked breath fogged up the glass. His right eye twitched. Dano wore an expression that Mayson had seen in the faces of jumpers and armed robbers pinned down by the cops.

Mayson tried to communicate with one glare, *stay cool,* but the dark of the moonless night swallowed up any nuance he could have conveyed without words. Without another glance to Dano, he trudged off in the direction the Vegan indicated, to a path behind the trailer. The trail was narrow between the rows of that strange crop and deeply shadowed. The stalks loomed twice as tall as the ones by the road.

Mayson paused right at the entrance. "I'm not going in there. I'll leave this on your porch."

"Please." The man's voice dripped with smarm. "I'm too

old and frail myself to carry such a thing. The pen is nearby. Just a few steps."

Mayson reassured himself with the steel presence of the Buck 616 in his hand. Part of him, he realized, wanted to see what shit was in this pen.

He stomped forward and the leaves slapped his boots. The trailer and the car vanished behind a curtain of vegetation, packed more densely than any corn maze he'd ever had the pleasure of getting lost in. Moreover, he was increasingly convinced it was not corn. The bulbs multiplied on the stalks and grew larger, purplish in the gloom, veined and rippled like obscene cabbage. Farther into the interior, the path opened up to a crop-circle-like arena, the stalks mashed down and brown at his feet, bulbs popped open like eggs.

More of a concern was the stone slab in the center of the clearing, a narrow rock with deep grooves worn into its surface and stains that shone black in the starlight. Mayson remembered a documentary with a similar thing. A stone to grind grain into a pulp. A metate. He remembered watching a person push grain about on the surface until it was broken and white.

On this particular stone, something deep red and dark had been pulped upon the surface, and Mayson did not care to know what.

Dull, white shapes were littered about the stone like the aftermath of some haphazard barbeque. Curved cages and a few calcified wings. After a moment, his vision adjusted to the dark and he could tell what those were. Mayson's gorge rose.

The Vegan moved behind him.

Mayson glowered, his body tense as knives. "I heard you didn't eat meat."

"I don't." The man gestured at the circle, and the shadows between the stalks quivered. "But they do."

Mayson squinted, but he could see little in the darkness between the stalks. The leaves twitched. Something moved inside. He had the sudden sense that the shadows were not shadows but instead another substance, like the surface of a brackish pond, and these were not rows of vegetation but instead a fence braced in front of the otherworldly muck, barely able to keep the carbon-black strangeness from slipping out.

Then something curled out from between the stalks. A finger of shadow.

The old man smiled behind him with a mouth of strange teeth. "You'll do well to place the package on the altar."

"I'm not placing shit," Mayson whispered.

"Don't make them come get it."

In the distance, Dano screamed.

The old man giggled, singsong. "Too late."

The leaves of the crop rustled, and the stalks parted, but Mayson had already crouched low and ready to bolt. Adrenaline shot through him, and a little, wild part of him screamed *don't look* at whatever crept out from the darkness. He caught, from the corner of his vision, something upright like a man but with proportions off, and he told himself *it's only tigers* before he chucked the cargo into the middle of the circle and booked it. The package landed and the blow tore apart its duct-taped black plastic. Cuts of grocery store beef scattered across the stone, but Mayson didn't stay to watch whether the horrible thing—*the tiger the tiger*—from the field stopped to investigate it.

Mayson ran and the old man blocked his path, but in a reflex Mayson lashed out with the 616 and something dark spilled from the man's spindly ribcage. Not a sound was made, but for the splatter of liquid onto the crushed stalks underfoot.

Mayson ran down the path and did not give any mind to his heart, which hammered as if about to explode. Just before he made it to the trailer, he heard the sedan's engine kick on and the tires spin in the gravel.

When he emerged from the path, he found the sedan in the middle of a three-point turn, with a tangle of activity behind the wheel. Dano flapped his arms madly as though harried by a wasp. He shared the car with a shadowed horror, which wrapped itself around him with long limbs. The attack interrupted Dano's maneuver and the sedan spun out, lurched forward, and slammed into the side of the rusted tractor.

The driver-side door flung open. By the time Mayson convinced his body to move—*breathe, dammit*—Dano had already been dragged out by the horrible thing. Mayson saw, in the spaces between heartbeats, a fan of sharp digits on Dano's torso and a splatter of black rain down the driver's seat. It happened quick. Mayson's brain spun and Dano looked to him like a rack of lamb. Spareribs. Organs tumbled out onto the ground like water balloons as the horror dragged the kid into the rows.

Mayson tried, he really tried, to lurch forward and grab the kid, but as soon as he swiped, his fist met air. From behind the stalks, Dano shrieked in repeated bleats and then the sound cut off sharply.

The stalks on the path rustled behind him. Mayson knew, although his brain scrambled to think of another explanation, more of the horrible things approached.

If he stopped to look at them for long—their limbs, oddly bent elbows and knees, the long faces with veins of dark popping out around bulbous skulls—he knew he'd lose his mind.

Instead, his focus landed on the sedan. It sat with its door open, key in the ignition.

Mayson collapsed into the seat, slammed the gear into reverse, and put pedal to floor.

The sedan lurched as though he'd backed over something lumpy and Mayson paid it no mind. He sped off down the gravel road, a plume of dust behind him, and only after he was a good ways away did he bother to snatch shut the door.

The stink of fetid compost and fear filled the car, and Mayson retched onto the floorboard. He wavered dangerously from shoulder to shoulder. When he righted himself, he kept his eyes on the road. Scrubbed his face. In the rearview mirror, he looked drained, phantomlike.

It was difficult to find the turn off from Butterbean Road, but when he saw the dark shape of the sign, he shoved the wheel right and the sedan lost traction. The skid warning light kicked on. Mayson managed to keep the lights pointed forward. As he drove wildly into the dark countryside, he did not look down at the silk and leaves strewn about the passenger seat.

He drove for over two hours, and exhaustion tugged at his limbs like concrete. The gravel road did not turn to blacktop and the city lights did not come into view. The night glittered with strange stars.

Mayson sweated and shook, and each time his thoughts attempted to return to what had transpired at the trailer, his head seemed to short out. He could only think of scenes from that tiger documentary. The slab of red meat laid before the grass. The way the stalks rustled. In the twist of his unraveled sanity, he saw on the slab, Dano's face, lit up green by the dashboard light. Dano, who no longer ate meat.

"That meat won't eat meat." Mayson said it to himself, and laughed stupidly for several minutes. "Hah! Ovo-lacto-nickto-verata!"

Mayson laughed and wept and nearly drove the car off the road a few times. The only thing that stopped him was the wall of leafy crops on either side. The highway had to be near. He was almost there.

After he'd driven even longer, the road came to a T.

There, on its post like the stem of a crooked flower, stood the sign. Butterbean.

From the passenger seat, Dano turned to Mayson and smiled grimly, his face pale green and drained of blood. A thin, mealy specter. The ghost's torso splayed open, his ribs fanned out like a rack of meat where the things had pried him apart.

The point was to take your ass out and leave you there, Dano said. *You think you'll make it back...*

Mayson wheezed behind the wheel. "I didn't summon you."

He kicked the gear into reverse and turned the sedan around, and the tires cast plumes of ghostly dust behind him. In the maneuver, the headlights came close to the stalks and for a moment cast what toiled inside them in sharp relief. More of those things writhed there in their carnivorous mimicry of vegetation, bulbous and unwholesome. Hundreds in a swarm.

With a cry, Mayson hauled the wheel and the tires kissed the road again. He hit the gas with a desperation that denied his new reality.

As he sped off into the night, he thought, *I just missed the turn*. Above him, the night smiled with stars.

GRIEF AND THE CARRION CROW

By Rob Francis

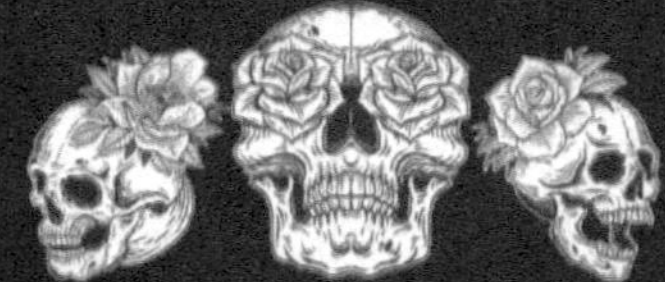

The old farm road is hostile to visitors, riddled with potholes and pinched so narrow it can barely accommodate the Jag. The bordering hedges are straggling hawthorn, near leafless this late in the year. They stand a little taller than I remember, but that's all. Everything else is the same. Nothing has moved on. Except for Keith.

At least big bro's at peace now, with Mum and Dad. As I drive, my eye catches him grinning at me from the order of service on the passenger seat. I turn it over and hold it against the seat as I jounce over another rut, but when I take my hand away it slips into the footwell and is lost amongst the mouldering debris of old magazines and food wrappers. I force myself to ignore it and focus on the road.

A dead badger sprawls by the verge, half-crushed, blood pooled dark about it. But who else has passed this way lately? There are no friends or family left to visit Andrew now, holed up alone at Crow Farm like a fox at bay. Only me.

Big sister and little brother. The family remnants.

It's been three years since we last met. But sales and acquisitions have their demands and London never sleeps. Time waits for no woman, as a more enlightened adage would have it.

My eyes dampen as I pass the old farm sign, cracked now, the wooden shingle split so that 'Crow' is neatly bisected. As I guide the Jag through the gate and into the yard, my stomach clenches. This place has changed since my last visit. In the worst possible way.

The farmhouse is almost unrecognizable. The walls are covered with ivy and brambles, as if the house itself is a vast, rotten egg in a bird's nest. The windows are so filthy that the interior of the house is hidden. The door, which I remember Mum painting a vivid scarlet back when I was just a budding teenager, is now bare wood, every inch of color scraped from it.

Across the yard, the barn roof sports a gaping hole. That must be where Keith fell through, to die amongst the old and rotten machinery. Other breaches amongst the tiles have been clumsily patched with dirty, blue tarpaulin.

Dad's tractor stands in one corner of the yard, half-covered by stands of buddleia and knotweed that have sprouted in a riot around it. The fields are choked with tall weeds; there are no signs of cows or sheep. A nebulous odor of decay rises from the ground itself.

This is an abandoned place.

I step from the car and, as I shut the door, a murder of crows erupts from the fields and swirls into the darkening sky. The crows have been there for as long as I can remember. For as long as anyone can remember.

I haul my overnight bag from the backseat and head for the front door. It opens before I'm halfway there, Andrew standing back a little from the weak daylight as if ready to retreat before he's even said hello.

"Andrew!"

I smile, but his shadowed face remains impassive. As I reach the door, he backs off. He is thin, painfully so, his skin washed-out and yellow-grey. He squints at me through filmy eyes. His hair is too long and matted with grease, so that it sticks out at odd angles. I can smell him from outside, the animal musk stink of sweat. When he finally speaks, his teeth—those that remain—are chipped and stained brown.

"Katie. I'm... I'm sorry I couldn't make it to say goodbye."

"Jesus, Andrew..."

The floor of the house is covered with debris, a hoard of junk that should have been thrown away years ago—yellowed newspapers, discarded bottles and food containers, broken furniture. The detritus of a failing life.

From the hallway, I can see into the kitchen and living room. Both look to be in the same condition.

"What's happened, Andrew? This isn't like you."

Tears stream down his cheeks as he nods, just once, before jamming his face in his hands. He sobs, body shuddering with each breath. I force myself to step close and fold my arms loosely around him. The smell almost makes me gag.

"It's okay, kid. What happened? Are you drinking again?" I can think of no other explanation.

"No. N-nothing like that." He wipes his eyes on a filthy sleeve. "It was Keith, he..."

Andrew tails off, then starts as if at a loud noise or a sudden thought. He turns and walks into the kitchen. I follow.

The clutter here is worse, if anything. Long-abandoned crockery is piled haphazardly across every surface apart from the kitchen table, which is patterned with dark stains. The floor is littered with old papers and rat droppings. The bin is full of small bones.

Andrew seems calmer here. He sighs. "Keith didn't cope so well, you know? Once Dad was gone."

Through the grimy windows I can just make out the edge of the barn roof, silhouetted against the setting sun. Bile stings my throat.

"I suppose I'm not surprised. Keith just about worshipped Dad. He was a complete wreck at the old man's funeral. So, what did he do?"

"Just let things go. Stopped looking after the place. Sold

the livestock, talked about selling the farm and moving away. He couldn't though, 'cos it belongs to all three of us. I told him that. Then he stopped going out, apart from the occasional deer shoot. For a while, I kept everything up as best I could. Drove to town to get the things we needed, when we still had the Ford."

He moves a stack of old papers from a chair so I can sit down, then switches the kettle on. "Tea?"

"Sure," I say, though I'm not. Anything prepared in this kitchen would pose a health risk.

He drops a dusty tea bag in a cup I hope is clean but know in my heart hasn't seen soap and water for an age.

"After a while I just...joined him, I suppose. Gave up. There didn't seem much sense in fighting. After a certain point, things get beyond repair."

"Why didn't you call me? I know Keith would've been too proud to ask for help, but not you."

"Always been the little brother, Katie, haven't I?"

"I don't mean it like that. Just—"

"I know, I know."

"I can understand why you didn't want to go, Andrew. Really."

"Was it a good service?"

"Just me and Father Clifford. A few words in the church, then out back for the lowering into the ground. You didn't miss much, though it breaks my heart to say so."

He nods as another tear slides down his cheek.

"Look, do you have anything to eat? For yourself, I mean. I have a few things in my bag that'll tide me over, and I assumed you'd have something in." I open my arms to take in the kitchen, the farm, his life. "But I guess..."

Andrew shakes his head. "I'm not all that hungry right now. The oven doesn't work in any case. I'll go out and get something later. Tomorrow maybe, after you've headed off. You're back at work Monday?"

"Actually, I have a couple of days off. I thought I should stay a night or two, see how you are. Maybe we can go shopping together in the morning, and then I can help you clean up a bit. You'll feel better once you make a start, you'll see."

"Yeah." He brightens a little. "Yeah, okay."

"I brought you this." I hand over another copy of the order of service I kept in my suit jacket. The cover bears an old photo of Keith, red-faced and grinning, from when he was in his mid-twenties and full of life. I told Father Clifford that's why I chose it. In truth, it was the most recent photo of him I had.

"Thanks." Andrew glances at it before putting it atop a pile of old magazines. He pours the tea and hands me the mug. I take it but don't drink. "Is he near Dad?"

"Next row back. Not that many people being buried at Saint Peter's these days."

He nods. "I'll get up there when I can."

I give him time, to see if he wants to say anything else. After a few minutes of silence, I give up.

"So, where am I sleeping? I'll go get changed. My old room still Dad's study, is it?"

Andrew shrugs and manages a watery smile. "More a storeroom now. You can sleep in Keith's room. I don't go in there."

I take my bag and the mug upstairs, stepping into the bathroom at the top of the landing to pour the tea down the sink. The wall and floor tiles are thick with mold, the bath crusted with brown scum. I turn the tap and am relieved to see clear water flow, washing the dark tea away. Mild poisoning averted, I step into Keith's room.

The sight of the skull is like a punch to the stomach and makes me halt in the doorway, gut hurting, heart in my throat.

It's above the bed, huge, elongated and grinning, two large naval cavities at the bottom and shadows darkening the orbits higher up. Two vast antlers project to brush against the ceiling, their color darker, an almost wooden red-brown.

A stag's head.

"Jesus."

I walk from the bedroom and peer into the others. Each one, even Andrew's, is crammed with junk. I return to Keith's room. This is the only one that is relatively neat and clean.

"No wonder you stay out of this room, Andrew," I whisper.

If I must sleep here, I resolve to at least make the best of it. I'm not prepared to sleep under the skull. Not only is its looming, skeletal sharpness disturbing, it's also bolted to the wall right above the bed, and I wouldn't trust it not to fall on me during the night.

No. Some alterations are needed.

I shove a small desk and a couple of boxes into one corner to make space, then drag the bed to the middle of the room. At least it's facing away from the skull, so I won't be able to see it if I wake in the night. I dig a pack of zopiclone from my bag for later.

I unpack some clothes and get changed, oddly shy in front of the grinning animal. Why the hell would Keith put that in his bedroom? I know he liked hunting, but still. It's horrible.

"Fuck you," I say, glaring at it. That helps.

Sleep eludes me, despite the zopiclone. I lie in Keith's bed, the musty scent of the sheets tickling my nose, and think on my awkward conversation with Andrew earlier in the evening. While we sat in the kitchen and I chewed my way through a couple of off-brand protein bars, and Andrew ate nothing at all, we'd reminisced about Keith. About growing up together in this house. But when I asked again how Keith had been before the accident, Andrew had clammed up.

Whoever my older brother had become in the years since Dad died, I didn't know him, and Andrew didn't want to talk about him.

I can't see the stag's skull from where I lie. I try not to think about it.

The medicine's beginning to work when I hear the scrape of movement downstairs, followed by the click of the front door. I cross to the window and look out on the yard. All is as it was when I arrived. The Jag waits where I left it, the moonlight shining off its polished frame.

And there is Andrew, shuffling to the gate and the road beyond.

I sit on the bed, thinking to wait for him to return so I can ask where he might have been going at three in the morning, but the sedative in my system pulls me down to uneasy oblivion.

A noise from the kitchen wakes me. For a moment, it's as if I'm a teenager again, woken in the early morning by Mum making breakfast. I can almost smell toast and eggs and coffee, can almost hear Mum and Dad talking, laughing, as they set the table. I lie half-awake until reality floods back in.

They are all dead, apart from me and Andrew.

And Andrew is back in the house.

I slip from the bed and pull on a pair of slacks, careful not to make much noise, resolutely turned away from the stag's empty gaze.

I creep down the stairs, remembering all the times I did so as a child to watch TV while Mum and Dad were sleeping.

The kitchen is dark but there is enough moonlight from the dirty windows to see Andrew hunched over the table, snarling like a feral animal, shaking his head from side to side as if tearing at something.

Holding as still as I can, I flick the light switch.

Andrew looks up in astonishment, blood and slime around his mouth. On the table, rent apart and half-eaten, lies a badger, fur and bones still clinging to torn lumps of meat and gristle.

It takes a moment for Andrew to focus on me. His breath hisses in the silence.

I can't move. I'm nauseated and exhausted and confused. I want to sleep and I want to run.

"What the fuck's going on, Andrew? You're eating, what, roadkill? Raw? What the absolute fuck?"

He wipes his mouth on the back of his hand like a child.

"Help me. Help me Katie, please." He points to the ceiling, to the room above. Keith's room. He lowers his voice. "It's her."

"What?"

"The deer. In Keith's room."

The nausea and fatigue intensify, the zopiclone still trying to shut my brain down for the night.

"What are you talking about? And that's a boy deer, Andrew. It's got huge antlers for fuck's sake."

"No, you don't understand. Keith went hunting, and he saw the deer, but... And he wasn't supposed to, he knew it was wrong, but he didn't care after Dad died and shot it anyway and brought it back here. We hardly ate any of it, I swear, and then Keith boiled the head down in the barn and put the skull up there on the wall. But it made her mad, Katie, really mad."

He motions to the badger's remains. "Now I can only eat dead things, like this. Nothing else will stay down." His eyes light up. "And it tastes so good."

"Don't talk so fucking stupid, Andrew." I'm breathing fast and hard, unsure whether to argue or run or slap his stupid face. I can't concentrate. I try to calm down and stay focused. "You're ill, Andrew. I see that now. You and Keith together.

You made each other worse somehow. Though I expect it was Keith getting to you more than anything. He always pushed you around."

"I can't help myself. I can't help myself, Katie. You don't understand."

"Please," I say, "can we just agree that you'll not eat any more of...that, and we can talk more in the morning?"

He looks at the half-eaten badger mournfully. "Sure, sis. Anything you say. I want to get better, I really do."

"Good."

Lightheaded, I clutch at the doorframe to keep from falling. Andrew sits at the table, head bowed as if awaiting punishment. I lean on the wall as I climb the stairs to Keith's room, still trying to make sense of what I've seen and what Andrew has said.

I lie down and give myself to sleep. But when it comes it is not the usual velvety blackness that envelops me, but the sepia grey of an old photograph. It forms an image of a woodland clearing, and I'm standing at the tree line, watching the long grass wave in the wind.

And a deer, a huge stag with tall, jagged antlers steps from the trees and into the open space, proud as a king. A naked woman sits atop him. Her skin is wrinkled and liver-spotted, breasts pendulous, stomach lined and round. She rides with legs astride the great deer's flanks, facing forwards but with her head turned away so that only a long, tangled mass of grey hair is visible, hanging almost down to the ground.

I don't want to see her face.

Yet I can hear her voice, like the keening of the wind through a ravine.

I choose the quarry.

I open my mouth but cannot speak.

The sun is bright, and I am standing on the dusty carpet in Keith's room, gazing up at the stag's skull. It's morning and I have no idea how long I've slept, if at all. My muscles ache and it's hard to move. And I'm hungry. Ravenous.

The house is silent. I step onto the landing and make my way to Andrew's room, to see if he is asleep. He isn't there. The bed is empty, the bedclothes crumpled against the headboard. All around the bed, the room is layered with the domestic debris that covers most of the rest of the house. It seems little more than a nest for a small animal.

As I turn to leave, I spy a mouse lying atop a pile of moldered clothes. It's been dead for a few days at least. The body is a little flattened, the grey-brown fur matted and twitching in places as tiny, white maggots do their work.

It smells delicious.

I mean to turn away but instead find myself lifting the tiny corpse by its tail and lowering it into my upturned mouth, letting it nestle on my tongue for a moment before biting into it, relishing the crunch as its miniscule bones surrender to my teeth. I'm reminded of childhood, the first time I tasted milk chocolate and honeycomb, the wonder of the flavors and texture. I chew and swallow. The sharp bones snag my gums and throat, but I've never tasted anything half as good.

"Katie?"

Andrew stands at the bedroom door. I turn away so he can't see me lick my fingers.

We sit at the kitchen table, the remains of the badger spread between us. I try to ignore the wonderful aroma, redolent of one of Mum's roast dinners. Andrew's eyes are black and sunken. I'm sure mine are too. He offers a weak smile.

"I saw you eat the mouse."

I don't know what to say.

He chews his lip, teeth dark against the pale skin. "You saw her, didn't you?"

"Who?"

"The old woman. The deer-herd." He lowers his voice. "She's still not satisfied. Even with Keith dead, it's not enough."

I'm too tired. I need to sleep. "What does she want?"

"I don't know. Damn Keith. He cursed us, bringing that stag home."

"Let's just leave," I say, though I make no move to do so. "You can come stay with me in London. I have space."

"I'm not sure."

He reaches out and for a moment I think he's going to take my hand, but instead his fingers come to rest on a scrap of badger leg, busy with tiny black flies. He pulls it towards him.

We stare at each other. My stomach growls.

"I'm sorry," he says, and slips the scrap into his mouth.

Moments later, I reach for the carcass too.

My stomach full, I can finally sleep. I doze all day, drifting in and out of dreams that I can't remember, each waking moment marked by waning daylight. Sounds draw me to temporary wakefulness—the crows in the fields, rain against the window, the rumble of car tires over uneven ground. Silence brings me back to my dreams.

Until it is night again, and I wake, starving and desperate. I stumble out of bed and down the stairs to the kitchen. If Andrew hasn't been to scavenge any food, I'll have to go myself.

But he's there, the table illuminated by candlelight, the candle itself standing in an old wine bottle next to something that I can't quite make out. I step into the kitchen, my feet slipping a little on fresh mud.

"Andrew?"

"Katie. I took your car. I hope you don't mind."

An old tea towel covers whatever is on the table. It looks taller than the badger, but not as long. The scent is different, and tantalizing.

"What is it?"

"I think I worked out what she wants."

He reaches out a dirt-covered hand and whips the towel away with a flourish.

Keith's face looks nothing like I remember. The head is almost fleshless, the skin tight across the skull, hair thin, one eye closed, the other half-open, mouth slack. It sits at an angle on the table, because Andrew has severed it from the body inexpertly so that part of the neck bone protrudes.

My mouth waters.

"Keith wasn't supposed to kill the stag. It hadn't been chosen, wasn't its time. But he shot it. Ate it. Mounted the head on his wall. Now she wants us to do the same to Keith."

I stare at my brother's head. It's all I can do not to take a bite.

Andrew lifts a carving knife. "Shall I?"

"Keith wasn't fixing the roof when he fell, was he?" I ask.

Andrew shakes his head. "He went to fetch the body of a crow that'd died up there. We were running out of food."

"And the roof just gave way?"

He nods and looks away. "I saw him heading for a weaker part, but I didn't say anything. I didn't want to. He'd cursed us, and I knew things wouldn't get better until... Until he'd gone. But then, after he'd fallen, I couldn't stand it. So I called for help. I'm sorry, Katie. But I wanted it to end. You can understand, can't you?"

He steps forward and puts a trembling hand atop Keith's crown, ready to begin carving. I reach out, unsure what to do, unsure whether I'm reaching for Andrew or Keith, to stop one brother or take a piece of the other.

My knuckles clip the wine bottle and it tumbles, candle flickering. It rolls off the table.

And lands in a stack of old newspapers.

The flames spread as if they have been waiting impatiently for their chance. For a second, both of us stare at the fire, wild-eyed. Then I turn and make for the door.

It's only when I'm standing in the yard that I realize Andrew isn't with me.

Flames rise in the dark kitchen windows. Smoke is pouring from the front door. I hesitate, telling myself that I'm ready to rush back inside. Any moment now.

Andrew's silhouette stands against the orange glow of the kitchen, unmoving, as if he is looking out at me, or perhaps back into the house. He raises a hand.

There is a terrible wail, a hideous screeching that rolls around the farm and sets the crows to flight in the night, their shapes stark and black against the moon. I can't bear it.

I run for the car. The keys are still in the ignition, Andrew having left them there on his return from the churchyard. The car seats are dark with earth, wetness soaking into my slacks as I sit and buckle myself in. I slam the door and turn the engine over, but don't drive away. Not yet.

Instead, I turn the radio up loud, so loud the music drowns out my thoughts. The house burns, blurred through the endless tears that run unchecked down my face to fall in my lap. The windows smash, flames licking at the sides of the house as they climb. The roof cracks, splits, and falls inwards, sending an eruption of smoke and sparks into the night sky. I fancy there are two huge shapes that emerge from the shattered shell of the house, black-winged birds with bodies of smoke, trailing fire as they leap into the firmament, circling around, weaving past each other, until I can't see them anymore.

I turn off the radio. The wailing has stopped. There is only the crackle of flames and the snapping of old, heat-twisted timbers.

I leave the Jag behind and bolt into the nearest field, pushing through the damp vegetation. The burning shell of my family home lights the ground, illuminating the shapes of animal bones and skulls scattered amongst the weeds. Sheep, pigs, cows. The farm's livestock, slaughtered here and left to rot. Picked clean by my brothers and all the other carrion crows.

I race across the bone-riddled earth as fast as I can, trying not to fall. Trying not to think.

I am the last of my family. A murder of one.

The crows follow me in the night, flying just above my head.

They laugh as they call my name.

FOX DEN

By Kay Hanifen

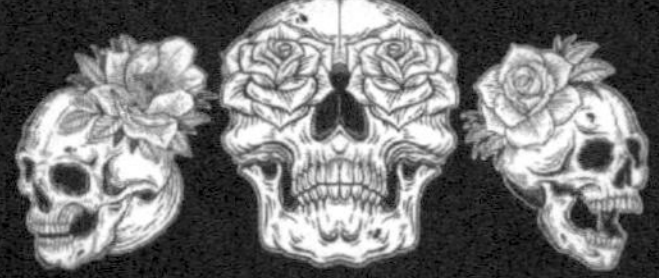

Jesse pulled up to the soundly shut, wrought iron gate separating the main road from the community of Fox Den. Her community. At least, it had been, but then life happened. She left home, attended college in the big city she loved against her parents' wishes, found a girlfriend, and, over time, the idea of returning to the old neighborhood became less and less attractive.

She took in a deep breath, inhaling the acrid smell of smoke that permeated the remains of her and Talia's possessions. It was a smell that refused to be suppressed, no matter how many times they washed them, or how many cans of Febreze they emptied in the car. If it were possible, they would've moved in with their friends, Maggie and Georgia, but they had disappeared months ago, leaving behind a note about going to stay with Maggie's family.

And now for another homecoming.

Seeing the look on her face, Talia reached over and squeezed her thigh.

Jesse let out a short, nervous laugh. "The prodigal daughter returns."

"Just until we get back on our feet."

"Right," she said, "alright." She rolled down the window, letting the crisp, October evening air briefly flush out the smell of smoke and the cloying scent of Febreze, and buzzed the intercom. "Jesse Harper and Talia Grayly here to visit the Harper family."

If there was someone on the other side of the intercom, they gave no acknowledgement. She sat back and exchanged glances with Talia. "That's weird. They told me we were on the list, but, I dunno... Traffic made us later than expected, but I still think they'd—" Slowly, the gates swung open. She blinked and Talia shrugged. "Okay, never mind then."

They drove through the neighborhood in silence, the hairs on her neck prickling. It was an all-too-familiar sensation—a feeling that had forced her to flee to a place of noise and people and constant motion—but it felt amplified somehow. It was as though the eyes that had watched her as she played in the streets and wandered the woods as a kid had multiplied.

She didn't know why she felt that way. By all accounts, the gated community was beautiful. Houses stood like handsome soldiers, uniform and in perfect, straight rows. Each had flowerbeds out front, with blooms somehow still vibrant in mid-October. Unlike before though, where the feeling of being watched could simply be chalked up to paranoia, the stillness was palpable, like the neighborhood was holding its breath. If there were any birds around, they must have settled in for the night and the wind had died, refusing to run though the leaves in trees aflame with autumn colors.

A flicker of movement drew her eye to one house. A pair of curtains flicked shut and all was still again.

"Was it always this dead when you lived here?" Talia asked.

She shook her head. "Things were quiet, but not this quiet. There were birds and kids staying out a little too late and...I dunno. It's just different. It's like everything is..."

"Waiting and watching us?" Talia finished for her.

"Yeah." She pulled into her parents' driveway and rubbed

her eyes. "I think we're just used to living in a city. All that motion and sound. It's just not like that here."

Talia sighed. "Probably. I think I'm just still on edge."

Jesse leaned over, resting her head on her girlfriend's shoulder. "Me too." She laughed to herself, a short, almost hysterical bark. "I mean, we just survived a fire with little more than the shirts on our backs. Of course we're on edge."

Their apartment had been their haven. It was the site of game nights and movie nights, of potlucks and dance parties. They decorated it with Jesse's art and filled the rooms with Talia's music. The fire that destroyed their apartment had cremated a part of Jesse too.

Talia kissed the top of her head. "Ready?"

She straightened up. "Twenty-five and moving back in with my parents."

"For now," Talia said.

"For now," she repeated and sighed, "We are so late. Mom's gonna kill me."

They grabbed the boxes of surviving possessions from the back and made their way to the front door, ignoring the prickling sensation on their necks. With a wave of dread, Jesse raised her hand to knock on the door.

Before she could, her mother opened it. She wore a big, toothy smile and pulled Jesse and Talia into a bear hug. "I'm so happy you're home!"

"Sorry we're late," she said. "You know how traffic is on the highway."

Her mother shook her head. "Don't worry about it, Jessica. I'm just glad you're here!"

Jesse blinked. "Oh. Okay."

Liz Harper was never one to mince words or hide her displeasure. She was a woman made entirely of sharp edges, with cheekbones that looked as though they could cut glass, severe grey eyes, and straw-colored hair pulled into a tight bun. By contrast, Jesse was round and soft—too round for her mother's taste—with light blue eyes and her father's brown hair.

But her mother's face and disposition had softened in the months since she'd last visited. When was it? Christmas? Whenever it was, her mother had admonished her for being late and letting the dinner get cold. This time, she ushered Jesse and Talia into the kitchen, scarcely giving them time to put down their things before shoving a hot plate of chicken marsala in front of them.

They exchanged surprised glances. With a shrug, Talia tucked in, and Jesse followed suit.

As she ate, she took stock of her mother's kitchen. It looked like it had been recently remodeled. Before, her mother had preferred a modern kitchen, with sleek and simple hardware and a design that favored utility over aesthetics. Now, it looked more like a farmhouse, with warm, cozy autumn colors. In fact, the whole house seemed decorated for Fall. Pumpkins lined the immaculate kitchen counter, and garlands of witches hung across the windows. A painting of a fox hung above the fireplace in the living room and another in the kitchen.

"It's nice to finally meet you, Mrs. Harper," Talia said, breaking the awkward silence. "I wish it could be under better circumstances, but we're so grateful you're taking us in."

"Please, call me Liz," Jesse's mother replied, straitening her prim, periwinkle dress. "All my girlfriends do. And you two can take all the time you need. You've both been through a lot, and I'm glad you found each other. Jesse's lucky to have a roommate like you."

Talia coughed and looked between mother and daughter quizzically. "I..."

Jesse squeezed Talia's hand, cutting her off. "She's my girlfriend, remember? We've been dating since sophomore year."

Her mother blinked, that plastered on smile faltering for a moment. "Oh, that Talia. I'm sorry. I have no idea why that slipped my mind."

Jesse put down her fork, a sinking feeling in her stomach putting her off food. "Hey, Mom, are you okay? You seem... different."

Her mother tilted her head in confusion, her smile again wavering. "I don't know what you mean. I'm fine! Better than ever!"

Jesse and Talia exchanged worried glances. Before she could press her mother any further, the front door opened.

"Hello?" her father called out from the foyer. "Anyone home?"

"Dad!" Jesse exclaimed, leaping to her feet and running into his open arms as soon as he entered the kitchen.

Mike Harper was aging into what her mother would call a silver fox. His thinning, dark hair and goatee had flecks of silver, and smile lines showed on his face. He still looked to her a bit like George Clooney. He wore his work suit, tie pulled loose but not entirely removed. After a moment, they parted.

When they did, she realized he had not returned alone. Behind him was a short, squat woman in her fifties with beady eyes and a penetrating gaze fixed on Talia. She looked vaguely familiar.

"You remember Mrs. Nesbitt, don't you?" her mother said.

"Of course, she does," Mrs. Nesbitt exclaimed, pulling Jesse into a hug that lasted a few seconds too long. After what seemed like an eternity, they parted and she said, "You don't forget your neighbors. It takes a village to raise a child, you know?"

"But we—" Jesse began to protest, but her mother cut her off.

"Of course she remembers! She and Brett were thick as thieves!"

She did remember the Nesbitt's...kind of. She went to high school with their son, but they were never close. In all honesty, he always struck her as a bit of a douche, flirting with every girl in his path, always smelling of beer and Axe Body Spray. But she wasn't about to set the record straight.

Her eyes met Talia's, and her girlfriend mouthed, *What is happening?*

She mouthed back, *No idea.*

Mrs. Nesbitt's gaze shifted over to Talia. She stared for a moment, something inscrutable flickering across her face. Then, her smile widened, and she asked, "And who's this?"

Talia crossed the room to take her place at Jesse's side.

"This is Talia. She's my—"

Once again, her mother cut her off. "Roommate. They've been rooming together since sophomore year."

She ushered the women to the kitchen table while Jesse's father took his place on the couch with the evening paper.

"Oh, then you must have lost your apartment in that awful fire too," Mrs. Nesbitt said.

Talia's face tightened with grief. "Yeah, it's hitting us hard."

"Do they know who set the fire yet?" Mrs. Nesbitt's eyes were bright with curiosity.

Talia blinked. "Uh, we don't know what caused the fire, but they ruled out arson. Why do you think someone set it?"

"Oh, you know how cities are," Mrs. Nesbitt replied, with a shrug. "Hoodlums and criminals everywhere. You know, I warned Jesse's mother all those years ago. Cities are not safe places for young women. You never know what's gonna happen. It's only a matter of time."

Talia let out a shocked bark of laugher. "You're kidding, right?"

Jesse could see the righteous fury building in her girlfriend like a volcano and knew it was best to change the subject before the eruption. "So, uh, Mrs. Nesbitt, what do you do?"

"Oh, I'm retired, dear. I recently took charge of the homeowner's association, just to entertain myself. Now, my only job is keeping this neighborhood beautiful and safe. Your father and I just came from a meeting. Isn't that right?"

Her father grunted from the couch. Before, he would have joined the conversation. Hell, he would have dominated it with stories and jokes and words of wisdom. But now he sat still on the couch as though oblivious to the women talking near him. That, too, worried Jesse. What was wrong with her parents?

"And you?" Mrs. Nesbitt asked, fiddling with the sleeve of her shirt as through trying to act thoroughly disinterested in the conversation. "What do you do in the city?"

Something told Jesse that Mrs. Nesbitt was *very* interested. In their limited correspondences since she'd moved out, her mother made Mrs. Nesbitt out to be quite the gossip. She collected information on each and every person in the neighborhood. If you wanted to know if your husband was having an affair, or your teenager was sneaking out, you went to her. Nothing seemed to escape her prying eyes.

She could feel Talia seething beside her. "I'm an artist and Talia's a musician. While we're establishing ourselves, I work as a graphic designer and she's a music teacher."

"How fascinating," Mrs. Nesbitt replied. She leaned in conspiratorially, staring at them with her piercing, beady eyes. "Any boyfriends?"

She sounded teasing, as though it was just a question between girls, but there was a subtext to it that Jesse didn't like.

Jesse forced a laugh. "No, no boyfriend. I've always been too busy for that."

"Honey, you can't just devote yourself to work," she chuckled, smacking her shoulder playfully. "You have to live."

"I will when I don't have to worry about rent," she replied, with near equal joviality, and squeezed Talia's hand under the table.

"I know it's not exactly twenty-first century of me, but that's exactly why you should get a boyfriend, Jessica. A real man will provide for you. Even if they're cheating like Mrs. Crenshaw's... Well, never mind. I probably shouldn't have mentioned it."

Jesse's jaw dropped, as did Talia's. She could hardly believe what Mrs. Nesbitt had just said. Talia was on the verge of laying into their new neighbor and, this time, Jesse wasn't going to stop her.

"Mrs. Nesbitt, that is one of the most—"

"Anyway," her mother interrupted sharply, "we have a long day tomorrow, don't we?"

"What's tomorrow?" Jesse asked, relieved by the change in subject.

"Didn't Liz tell you?" Mrs. Nesbitt asked. "Tomorrow's our annual harvest festival. You're welcome to come. It's the highlight of the year."

"Of course they're coming!" her mother said. "Even if I have to drag them kicking and screaming."

"Everyone will be so excited to see you," Mrs. Nesbitt said, standing up. "It was a pleasure seeing you again Jessica, and wonderful meeting you, Talia."

With that, she left.

"Well, you must be exhausted," Jesse's mother said. "I've prepared your room for you."

Jesse's bedroom was exactly how she remembered it. Stuffed animals stood guard on her bed, and her artwork adorned the walls beside band merch and movie posters. The only difference was a pair of white dresses laid out on the bed. She moved them to a nearby chair.

"So, this is your bedroom," Talia said, setting down their surviving possessions. "It's cute."

Jesse laughed as she shut the door behind her. "Thanks, I guess."

"You guess?"

She sighed and sat on the bed. "I mean, it's not really home to me anymore. If it ever was."

Talia sat beside her, slipping Jesse's hand in hers. "What do you mean? I mean, I know your parents can be harsh, but you always made it sound like normal, only-child frustrations. Why were you so nervous about coming back?"

She chewed her lip. "I'm going to sound crazy."

"I don't think you can sound any crazier than what I saw tonight."

Jesse took a deep breath, her light blue eyes meeting Talia's dark brown. "You remember that feeling you had when we drove through the neighborhood? That feeling like you were being watched and whoever was watching didn't like what they saw?"

Talia snorted. "I'm gay and black. That's, like, my default in places like this."

Jesse, too, chuckled. "Fair point."

"But, it's not a good feeling."

She shook her head. "No. No, it isn't. It's been like that since forever and I never really understood why. I still don't. All I know is that I shouldn't be here. This neighborhood and I are fundamentally incompatible." She rubbed her eyes. "Before I left for college, I had nightmares almost every night. The same one over and over again."

"What about?" Talia asked, putting an arm around her girlfriend's shoulder.

"I'm lost in the woods. Fox Den is almost entirely surrounded by a fence, so it's not that far of a walk to get to the edge of the neighborhood, but it feels like I've been wandering for hours. And there's something watching me, just out of sight. I can feel its hot breath on my neck, but I don't dare to look. Eventually, I reach a clearing with a stone table in the center. And, suddenly, I'm exhausted. It takes all my strength to get to that table and lie down. And that's when the thing that's been watching me strikes. I don't see it, but I feel its jaws on me, crushing bone and organs, consuming me from the inside out. And then I wake up."

"That's terrifying," Talia said softly, "You said it was before college…"

"As soon as I left home, they stopped." She shrugged. "I figured it was just my paranoia and stress over school and parental expectations affecting my subconscious. I still had them sometimes, when I come home for the holidays, but as I got older and made my own life, they faded along with that watched feeling. At least, they did until tonight."

"Yeah," Talia said. "You wanna talk about that? Because I am so confused. You always made your mom out to be the Wicked Witch of the West, but she was…nice? I guess? But I'm getting major Stepford vibes from her. I don't like it."

"Same!" Jesse leapt to her feet and paced the room. "Like, she sounded funny on the phone when she offered to let us stay here, but I figured she was just worried when she heard about the fire. Getting here, though, it's like my mom got a personality transplant after last Christmas. And how did she forget about you? Believe me, I haven't made our relationship a secret. I came out to both of them at sixteen. I went to prom with a girl. It took them a while to come around, but I thought they both had. It makes no sense." She let the sinking feeling in her stomach drag her back down onto the bed. "I-I'm worried about her. There's something seriously wrong going on here."

Talia chewed her lip. "These are your parents, so I'll let you take the lead on this. I'm not sure if I feel safe here, but if you want to stay and try to help them, if you think they need helping, I understand. And I'll do it with you. But unless we get a good explanation for the weirdness, I think I'm gonna look into some nearby motels that we can stay at instead. It might be harsher on our wallets, but—"

Jesse cut her off. "No, I think you're right. I need to figure out what's going on with my parents, but, yeah, from a safe distance. How about we find a motel tomorrow? Or maybe some friends will let us crash for a little bit."

"Sounds like a plan." Talia yawned. "But as soon as someone mentions a Sunken Place, I'm running. And I'm leaving you behind."

Jesse laughed. "Fair."

The smell of smoke that still permeated their belongings once again filled the room. Talia stood. "You mind if I open the window? I just can't stand the smell...and the memories."

Jesse absently waved her hand to say go ahead. She was lost in thought, worried about her parents and strung out by the stress of the past few days. She was also exhausted. Despite the earliness of the hour—her phone said it was only 22:00—she could barely keep her eyes open.

Talia, too, was yawning. She laid down next to Jesse, and neither bothered to change, brush their teeth, or even turn out the light.

Jesse woke to a cry in the night. It sounded like a woman in unimaginable pain. It was also...familiar. Like she'd heard it a long time ago.

Talia was awake beside her, eyes wide.

"What is that?" she whispered.

For several, terrible seconds that seemed to stretch into hours, they clutched each other and listened to the screams. Judging by the sound, it was close. Practically below her window. She knew she'd heard it before, but where?

In a flash of memory, she recognized the sound as one she heard often in January when she stayed out too late. Her breathing slowed and she relaxed, laughing a little to herself.

"It's just a fox. It's a mating call. They don't call it Fox Den for nothing." She climbed out of bed and closed the window. "It's weird though. I've never heard one in October before. Their mating season is in January."

Talia yawned, already drifting back to sleep. "Yeah... weird."

Jesse crawled into bed again and closed her eyes, but sleep didn't come to her as readily. She must have drifted off, because she had troubled dreams. The same dream of the woods and the eyes and the altar. She woke again a few hours later and slipped out the room and downstairs into the kitchen for a glass of water. Her mouth felt like cotton. She yawned and searched the kitchen for the new cup cabinet.

"Next to the sink," her mother said.

Jesse yelped, heart pounding. Once she recovered herself, she asked, "Sorry, did I wake you?"

Her mother, wearing a bathrobe, leaned against the wall. She was looking past Jesse, out the windows to the woods beyond. "No, you didn't wake me. The foxes..."

Jesse laughed. "They scared us too. Not quite their mating season, is it?"

"I don't think they're after mates," she replied absently.

This was her chance. Just her and her mother. No Talia, no neighbors, no father. No one her mother had to put on a performance for. She steeled herself. "Mom, seriously, are you okay?"

She still didn't look at Jesse, instead staring blankly into the darkness beyond. "I'm fine."

"You aren't *acting* fine. It's like you're a completely different person."

Her mother's eyes snapped from the window to her, face hardening. "You're the one who always said I was too harsh. That I wasn't fair to you. So, I'm trying to be better. You could have died for God's sakes!"

Jesse took a step back. "Alright, fair. But still..." She

gestured to the newly remodeled kitchen. "This isn't you."

Her mother crossed her arms. "According to the homeowner's association, the houses in Fox Den all need to have a certain aesthetic to them. They're supposed to feel homey and welcoming. My old kitchen was functional, but you remember how stark it was before. I just wanted everyone to be more comfortable."

She blinked. "I thought the homeowner's association only cared about the outside."

Her mother crossed her arms. "No, Mrs. Nesbitt believes that a home's beauty is created from the inside out. And I've come around to her way of thinking."

"And why were you so weird around Mrs. Nesbitt anyway? Like forgetting that Talia and I are together, and agreeing that I was close to her son when you know I didn't even like him." Jesse grabbed a cup from the cabinet and filled it with water from the sink.

"Mrs. Nesbitt has a lot of control in this neighborhood," she replied. "It's best to stay on her good side." That same empty smile as before returned to her face. "Besides, you and Brett *were* thick as thieves, as kids at least. You drifted apart in high school, but I promise you that you were friends."

Jesse shook her head. "I have no memory of that."

"The older we get, the foggier our childhood memories become. As to forgetting your girlfriend again, Mrs. Nesbitt is very traditional. I didn't know how she'd react to you two."

"So, homophobic. Okay."

Her mother's eyes widened.

"What? It's true, isn't it?"

She shook her head. "Be careful what you say, Jessica. Ears are everywhere."

"So, you want to protect your reputation over your daughter?"

Her mother's face hardened. "No! Look, everything I do, I do for you."

"Right, right, okay." Jesse rubbed her eyes again, suddenly exhausted. "I can't believe I'm saying this, but I'm starting to miss Stepford Mom. What about the first time you forgot about my relationship with Talia?"

Her mother looked beyond her, face once again becoming distant, and that toothy smile returned. "I don't know what to tell you. I forgot. As soon as you reminded me, I remembered everything, but it honestly slipped my mind."

Jesse stepped in front of her, so that her mother had nowhere to else look. "Which brings me back to my first question. Are you really okay? Have you ever had a memory lapse like that before?"

"Are you implying that I have early onset Alzheimer's or something?"

She looked offended. Offended was good. Better than that distant, too-wide smile.

Jesse shrugged. "Your words, not mine."

"Well, I don't. I'm sharp as ever."

"I only ask because I'm worried."

"It's not me you should be worried about," she muttered darkly.

Jesse blinked. "What do you mean?"

Her mother looked at her like she'd grown two heads. "The fire? You know, the thing that took your home and most of your belongings."

Jesse's eyes narrowed in suspicion. She clearly wasn't talking about the loss of her apartment, but she was too tired to press it. "Right, right, the fire."

Her mother snorted and turned to go back upstairs. "Now who's forgetting stuff?" She yawned. "I'm going back to bed. You should rest too. Tomorrow's gonna be a long day."

Jesse finished her water. She wasn't satisfied with her mother's answers, but for better or worse, she was acting a little more like her old self. Not exactly, but more than before. One thing was for certain, she wouldn't be solving that mystery before dawn, so with a yawn, she made her way upstairs and back into bed.

Jesse and Talia woke the next morning to a flurry of activity. The denizens of the neighborhood were busying themselves with setting up for the block party, setting up stations for food, drink, face painting and flower crown making among other attractions. A maypole had been erected at the center of the cul-de-sac, near the new homeowner's association headquarters, streamers fluttering in the breeze. Children carried around scarecrows and chased each other in homemade fox masks. In fact, much of the décor for this harvest festival was fox-themed.

She supposed it made sense. This was Fox Den, after all.

After watching from the windows for a few moments, Talia asked, "Did you ever have harvest festivals growing up?"

She shook her head. "Nope. We had Halloween parties but nothing like this. Must be a new neighborhood tradition."

"I don't like it. It's creepy."

Jesse sighed. "Tell me about it. We should find that motel fast."

"Good morning!" her mother called from the kitchen as the two made their way down the stairs.

A delicious smell wafted from the oven as her mother frantically baked pumpkin bread. Plates already covered the counter, slices artfully arranged and stacked in circles with additional spreads in the center.

When Jesse saw the plates and the bread already in the

oven, she whistled. "You've been busy."

"Your mother loves her pumpkin bread," her father said from the couch, not looking up from the newspaper in his hands.

"I'm feeding the whole neighborhood," her mother retorted, as she pulled out another loaf of pumpkin bread. "We can't have a harvest festival without pumpkin bread."

"If you say so."

She shoved a piece in both of their hands. "Here. Try. It's an old family recipe."

"You never used to make old family recipes," Jesse said, between bites. "You always said it would make me fat."

"Empty nest syndrome makes you do crazy things," she replied. "I found grandma's old recipes, Gods rest her, and thought I'd try something new. Turns out I love baking." She looked the two of them up and down, and that good, old distaste that never failed to make Jesse feel small appeared in her eyes. This time, though, her smile did not fade as it had in years past, instead becoming forced. "Is that what you two are wearing?"

She looked down at her burgundy sweater and jeans. "What's wrong with it? I mean, our options are kind of limited right now."

"It's just not what we normally wear to our festivals. Didn't you see what I left in your room?"

In truth, Jesse had discovered the white dresses laid out on her bed the night before. There were a lot of things she could have said about them. That dresses weren't their thing. That it looked like they were several sizes too big. That it was cold out and the dresses looked like they couldn't hold up against a gentle breeze. Eventually, she settled on, "I didn't realize they were for us. More to the point, you've had other festivals?"

Her mother rolled her eyes. "One for spring and one for summer. But that's not important. Can you two *please* change into those dresses?"

The 'please' was more an order than a request.

Talia turned to her and shrugged. "When in Rome, I guess."

Jesse sighed and resigned herself to a cold, oversized dress.

By the time they'd changed and tailored the dresses with safety pins so they didn't look like children playing dress up, the festival had begun. She, Talia and her mother carried out the plates of pumpkin bread and set them down in the baked goods booth run by a neighbor.

"There you are!" Mrs. Nesbitt exclaimed, beckoning them toward a group of neighborhood elders. They ceased their quiet conversation to stare at Jesse with pleasant smiles, unnerving in their emptiness. "We were wondering when you'd show. Jessica, you remember my husband, and Mister and Mrs. O'Doherty."

She nodded, introduced Talia as her roommate, and they made their polite greetings. In truth, she did not remember Mr. Nesbitt, or Mr. and Mrs. O'Doherty, but it was just better to pretend that she did.

"And my son, Brett, should be around here somewhere." Mrs. Nesbitt's head bobbed like a snake as she searched the crowd. Finally, her face lit up and she pointed to a booth providing hard apple cider. A group of young men gathered around it, drinking and flexing. "There he is."

Brett Jesse *did* remember. He'd been in her class in senior year, and strutted around the halls like a rooster, pecking on those who didn't immediately show deference. Eventually, he went off to some prestigious university to study business—why was it guys like that always seemed to study business?—and Jesse's mother had turned this into yet another failing to lay at Jesse's door. Even now, Brett was at the center of the group, flexing and crowing.

Mrs. Nesbitt sighed affectionately. "I always thought you two would make a good pair. I hope you do soon."

It took most of Jesse's willpower not to make a face at the idea.

Talia snorted and elbowed her. "I think you're right. They'd be perfect for each other."

Mrs. Nesbitt pushed her in his direction. "Thank you, Talia. Jesse, you should go get yourself a drink and talk to him."

"Yeah," her mother said sternly, "you should go. Have a drink."

She took Talia's arm. "Yeah, let's." Once they were out of earshot, she whispered, "Was that because you're upset that I didn't introduce you as my girlfriend? I just wasn't sure if it was safe."

She shook her head, laughing. "I get it. Not mad, just messing with you. Shit's weird. Safety first. So, let's get that drink. I have a feeling I'm gonna need it."

Jesse pointedly refused to make eye contact with Brett or his mother as the neighbor running the booth poured them drinks.

Talia pulled out her phone to look up motels nearby. After a few seconds, she groaned and said, "I'm not getting signal. I'm gonna walk around a bit, see if it improves. How about you play Nancy Drew? Figure out what the hell is going on here while I plot our escape."

Jesse nodded. "Sounds like a plan. Just stay in view. We don't wanna get too separated."

As she sipped her drink, she watched the uptight suburbanites let loose with booze and masks. Without the inhibitions of sobriety and visible faces, soccer moms flirted openly with men who were clearly not their husbands, and all-American dads strutted and pulled increasingly dangerous stunts. One pulled out an aerosol can and a lighter and used the fire to cook a kabob, much to the amusement of those around him. To them, it was even funnier when the fire lost control and scorched a mailbox. It was mesmerizing.

A tap on her shoulder pulled her from her reverie. She turned, expecting Talia with a cheap motel on her phone screen, but it was Brett.

"Hi Jessica," he said.

"Actually, it's Jesse," she replied, painting on a smile and sipping her cider.

He blinked. "Oh, I just thought... Because Liz always called you Jessica..."

"She just hates Jesse because I spell it like a guy, so she refuses to call me by it," she replied, with a bitter laugh.

"Anyway, Jessica, I heard about the fire, and I just wanted to say I'm sorry for your loss."

"Thanks. It's been rough."

He leaned against the booth. "Are you staying long?"

She shrugged. "Probably not. We just need to find a reasonable apartment."

"Are you sure?" he asked, "I mean, two young women, alone in the city..."

"I actually prefer it there," she snapped.

He blinked. "You do?"

"Cities are honest. You know what you're getting into. For every modern marvel, there's a trash-strewn alley, a piss-covered doorstep, the ambient smell of sewage in the air. Unlike small towns and suburbia, it doesn't hide its rot behind quaint pleasantries. And it's far less paranoid, no longer clinging desperately to an American dream that never truly existed."

He laughed. "Gee, tell me how you really feel."

"Sorry," she said, shaking her head, "I've just been hearing it a lot lately, and I lost my home. So, forgive me for not wanting to hear how dangerous it is."

"I understand. It really is a shame though. Did they catch the arsonist?"

She laughed in disbelief. "What arsonist? Why do people keep assuming it was an arsonist?"

"I just heard it through the grapevine," he replied with a shrug. He stepped in a little closer. A little too close for her comfort. "But, anyway, if you ever want me to show you around..."

"I've lived here my whole life. I think I'm good."

"Things have changed. My mom and the rest of the homeowner's association really made this place into something special. You should see our new headquarters. I can take you."

She shook her head and scanned the crowd for Talia, but she was nowhere to be found. "I'm good. My roommate and I wanted to wander the old neighborhood for a little bit."

Where was she? It was as though Talia had vanished into thin air.

"Really, I insist," Brett said, grabbing her arm.

She jerked it away. "And I insist you let me go."

With that, she stormed off. Talia couldn't have gotten far. She headed towards her parents' house, figuring that Talia had gone back there for the Wi-Fi. The house, though, was quiet.

"Talia?" she called out from the front door. No response. She moved deeper inside. "Talia? You in here?"

When she reached the kitchen, she saw something move in the woods outside the window. Then she heard a scream.

"Talia!" she exclaimed, running into the backyard. "Talia, where are you?"

Another scream, this time from deeper in the woods, and a flicker of white moving through the trees. She took off in pursuit, but no matter how far she ran, she couldn't seem to catch up.

The feeling of being watched grew. She could feel the eyes burning on her neck. The trees closed in around her. She'd been running for too long. She should have reached the fence that surrounded the community, but all she could see were trees afire with autumn leaves and dying undergrowth.

Another flicker of white out of the corner of her eye and she turned to follow.

She felt like a hunted rabbit, but she had no choice but to keep running. Talia was in danger. She had to find her.

Finally, Jesse found Talia stopped dead in a clearing. Her back was to Jesse, who stood, struggling to catch her breath.

"What's wrong?" she gasped, leaning against a tree. "Where'd you go?"

The world spun around her, and everything sounded like it was under water.

Talia said nothing. She slowly turned around and…

It wasn't Talia. It looked like her, but Talia's eyes were kind and playful, her smile warm. When this…thing smiled, its eyes were too wide and too empty, and it had too many teeth. Its smile just seemed to grow and grow beyond human capacity, its teeth too big and too yellow. It raised a too-long, too-bony finger and beckoned her closer.

"Where's Talia?" she demanded, but it said nothing.

She took one, tottering step forward. There was something…something in the food and drink. She was tired, so very tired, but she knew she had to stay awake. If she slept, she would never wake up. She took another step and the thing that looked like Talia vanished, leaving only the dress the real Talia had worn behind.

Jesse stumbled to it and clawed at it like it had answers as to where her love had gone, but it yielded nothing.

"Jesse," her mother said, from behind her. "It's time to come home."

"Mom, I don't understand. What's—?" Before she could finish her sentence, her mother forced a drink to her lips. She sputtered, coughing up cider. "What the hell was that?" she demanded, wiping the stinging alcohol from her eyes and leaping to her feet.

"It's for you own good. He provides for us. Keeps us safe. You'll never have to worry about money or food or homes."

She backed up. "What? You mean Dad?"

Her mother laughed. "No, honey, not your father. Though

he wants this too. We want what's best for you."

A small crowd emerged from the trees. Brett and his drinking buddies. The O'Dohertys. The Nesbitts. Her parents. Others she didn't recognize. They were eerily still, like foxes preparing to pounce on an unsuspecting rabbit.

"Then what the hell are you talking about?"

"He who walks within the woods," Mrs. Nesbitt exclaimed. She had changed into long, red robes that reminded Jesse of a Catholic Cardinal. The crowd tittered in agreement. "He who provides and keeps us youthful and safe. He who forges us into perfection. He brought you here, willing the fire in your apartment, so that you could become my son's bride."

"You...? *You* set the fire?"

She backed away slowly from her mother and the Nesbitts, but she was surrounded. She had nowhere to go, and she was so dizzy.

"It was for your own good," her father said, as he emerged from the trees, "Now you'll be safe from the outside world. You will be made perfect."

"Where's Talia?" she asked, scanning for an opening.

"She is one with Him, now and forever a guardian of the woods," Mrs. Nesbitt said.

"You killed her," she whispered, the sudden onset of grief almost bringing her to her knees.

But she stood firm, and as Mrs. Nesbitt exulted this 'He' without giving any useful information, claiming that they somehow honored Talia by letting 'Him' take her, she found her opening. One of Brett's drinking buddies had enjoyed just a little too much of whatever was in the cider. She bolted, throwing Talia's dress in his face before ducking under him.

The forest was impossible to navigate. She should have been heading towards the front of the development, but the trees just got thicker and the spinning in her head made it impossible to think straight. Eventually, she broke free and into the cul-de-sac. At the end was a building—the HOA headquarters.

In front, the harvest festival had become a mad bacchanalia of blood and sex. Men fought one another for women as orgies started on the front lawn. An old man fell over dead, and a group moved to devour him, feasting with inhuman teeth. Some chanted in a language she didn't understand, and the air crackled with energy that the headquarters seemed to be absorbing. She fell to her knees, the dizziness of the drugs overtaking her.

Once again, the Homeowner's Association surrounded her. She forced herself to look at her parents. "Mom, Dad, whatever creepy cult you've joined, I don't want to be part of it. Please. Let us go."

"I'm afraid we can't do that," Mrs. Nesbitt said.

As if on silent orders, Brett and his drinking buddies stepped forward. "I look forward to becoming one with you," he said, as he yanked her to her feet.

She struggled against him as he dragged her into the new headquarters. It was built more like a church than a municipal center, with pews carved in a dizzying pattern and tapestries of a foxlike being hunting incomprehensible monsters. At the center was an alabaster altar. They bound her to the altar as her parents, the Nesbitts, and the O'Dohertys chanted around her. The celebration grew louder and wilder as their chants reached a fever pitch.

And then, she felt His presence by the altar.

It wasn't a physical manifestation. More a sensation of something beside her. He sniffed around her like a curious dog. The image of a fox came to mind, one that saw her more as prey than a threat. It wasn't a fox, she knew, but that was the form it took. She also knew that if she saw His true form, she would go mad trying to comprehend Him.

And then He was in her, and He devoured her, transforming her into their desires.

Jessica Harper-Nesbitt had always preferred the suburbs. Cities were too loud and dangerous. Fox Den though, was paradise.

She lived there with her husband Brett, both sets of parents right next door. She devoted herself to Him, watched her figure, and made friends with the wives of Brett's drinking buddies. As a newcomer to Fox Den, it was nice to have friends.

She and Brett had been talking about having children. She looked forward to having a daughter.

She didn't know why, but she longed for a Talia.

GREEN

By Derek Heath

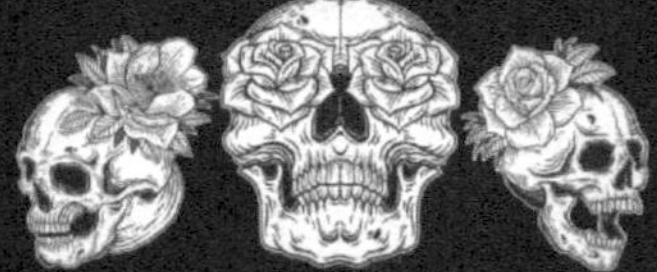

The forest bristled with life as she tumbled through it, half-running, half-staggering, the bundle of burlap gripped tight against her chest. It had stopped wriggling. Roots and ragged, wormy branches clawed at her feet, and tangles of thicket grabbed her ankles and threatened to throw her into the crawling undergrowth.

Ducking under a hanging oak branch—a limb severed from its trunk by what could only have been a bolt of lightning, dangling only from a knot of black, twisted wood—she chanced a look back into the dappled amber of the forest behind her. Nothing. Perhaps he'd given up. She clutched the still-warm bundle to her breast and scanned the trees, looking beyond them to the wheat-fields that crackled and bent in the wind. Peering between tall, thick pines and into the dark.

He was gone. He was gone. She was—

Crack!

The blast of the shotgun echoed, made her head pound. Ears ringing. The oak tree beside her exploded; chunks of rich, brown bark showered the earth at her feet. Shocked, she stumbled back, ankle catching on a thick, gnarled root of that same gargantuan tree.

Tripped.

The bundle fell from her arms and into the dirt as she stumbled to right herself. The two pheasants she'd wrung from her traps slid out of the burlap bag and gawped silently at her from the muck, throats tight, eyes wide and terrified. She bent down, reaching desperately for them, for the only thing that would keep her and the children fed over the next couple of days. For her livelihood.

She froze. Saw him in the shadows, barely thirty yards away. He was not the same man she'd seen out in the wheat-field, the big, pot-bellied man in the lumberjack shirt that she'd run from in the first place. This pale, shuddering figure was younger, scrawnier, brandishing a shotgun in one arm and a long-handled axe in the other. He grinned at her, mouth ripping open to flash rows and rows of tombstone teeth. He was naked, his flesh soft and pink and clinging to his bones.

Slowly, with a single arm, he raised the shotgun and pointed it at her face. Her eyes widened.

Crack!

She was already running when she realized a sliver of shrapnel from the shotgun blast had sliced through her calf. Warmth spread across her leg and trickled down her heel. Gluey, deep red drops beaded from the welt and scattered the forest floor behind her as she hurtled on, the pheasants abandoned, forgotten.

She ran with the wheat fields on her left, separated from the woods by a three-foot fence of barbed wire. She had thought the 'We Will Prosecute' sign meant they would get the police involved, but god, they were trying to kill her. They were *actually* trying to kill her.

She glanced out into the fields now and saw a dark smudge walking parallel with her. A dark smudge in a lumberjack shirt. Powerful strides carried the huge figure forward with a surprising grace; he kept up with her easily. His hands were empty, but she was more frightened of the heavyset man than she was of the scrawny bastard with the gun.

She had seen what he'd done to the last poacher caught out here.

She turned, hobbling away from the fence, aware that the farther she ran, the deeper into private land she came. There was no turning back now, not with what she assumed was the huge man's son in the woods with her. The only way was forward. Find somewhere to hide, to wait, then don't make a fucking sound—

Downhill. She was running downhill, and the trees were thinning, separating from each other, thick bands of daylight forcing them apart. She could hear frogs croaking, dozens of them, their combined chirping a rumble of lurid madness. The green cracked open and she saw fire, the blazing hot gold of the sunset as ribbons of pink were sucked into the horizon and split open, erupting into shards of purple and ripped-up red.

Colors surrounded her as she fell out of the woods and into a meadow. Tall wild grass danced madly around her as the sickly breeze that had trickled weakly through the forest turned to a stream of crashing, powerful wind that almost knocked her over. She was caught in a funnel.

Ahead, she saw a mess of thatch, a wide expanse of rotten, wet reeds, and over to the right, across an unkempt patch of wildflowers and grasses, the house. An old, crumbling farmhouse that had once been painted red, now bleached and drained by sunlight and the years to an awful, fleshy pink.

She turned to look over her shoulder. No movement behind her in the trees that climbed and bent up the hillock. No sign of the giant in the lumberjack shirt or the naked imp that she presumed was his son. Now was her chance.

She bolted.

Blood spat from the wound in her calf as she headed for the thatch. She could hide there awhile, wait for dark, wait for them to call it a night and then run back through the woods. They wouldn't actually kill her. They couldn't. If anything, those shotgun blasts had been a warning, and his grazing her calf an accident.

But he was naked. And the look in his eyes, that horrible grin…

He was fucking insane. They both were.

The chirruping of frogs grew louder as she neared the reeds, a screaming, crackling electricity that thrummed through the air. She saw slices of blue-grey between knots of thatch and figured the reeds must surround a pond of some considerable size. As she staggered closer, she caught an upwind whiff of the sour, hot smell of the water. Carbon dioxide and hydrogen sulfide breaking up beneath the surface; bad meat and eggs above.

She staggered into the reeds and paused, catching her breath. Turned, looked back. The two men were gone, and the forest was a blotted mass of darkness on the hillside. She stepped back, stepped back—

Her hip bumped something solid and sharp. She jolted, wheeled around, reeds scratching at her neck and back, and looked up.

A digger, parked leerily in the reeds—no, not parked, but abandoned, left here—with its bucket hanging into the water. Thick, black muck spilled out over the scoop's metal teeth. Rust sprayed the yellow walls of the cab, and she could see inside through greasy, smeared windows. The machine was huge, and she wondered how sunk into the boggy earth it must be for her to have missed it before.

She grunted, reaching up, grabbing for the doorhandle. She couldn't hide in here, that was too obvious—if they figured she'd come to the pond, this would be the first place they'd look—but perhaps there was something inside she could use to defend herself.

"Come out, come out, little chicken!" came a reedy voice from the meadow. It carried oddly on the wind, at once both strangled and screaming.

She swallowed as the door swung open and climbed inside the cab.

The seat was sunken, the wheel snapped off, leaving a sharp cylindrical mound jutting from the dash. The levers were rusted in place. She moved awkwardly between the seat and the footbed, looking for something she could snap off, something she could break.

"Oh, chiii-iiicken!" called another voice. Female.

She kicked at one of the levers, hoping it would come loose. It bent in the middle but didn't break off. She winced, kicking out again—

Something moved in the reeds, just outside the cab window. A flash of shadow. The smell of damp earth. She clamped a hand over her mouth, froze in place, refused to breathe, to move, to look. It was the imp from the woods, the wretch with the shotgun and the axe. She knew it.

"Come out, chicken..." he whispered, and his voice was behind her.

Slowly, she turned her head. The glass above her was pink with smeared blood, grains of dirt sprayed across it. Thatch batted at the window outside. Nothing there. Nobody. She turned back—

And the door swung shut.

She screamed as the giant in the lumberjack shirt pressed his face against the glass. His eyes were dead—not just cold and emotionless but long sapped of any life at all, grey and hollow and rheumy. He was massive, and bending down just to look in at her through the window. Slowly, he smiled, a thin crack splitting his stubbled, loose-skinned face wide open.

Oh god, it really was.

His mouth was stitched shut, thin, black ribbon curling through his lips, pressing them together. As his tongue pushed through, miniscule rivers of blood drizzled from the stitches.

A groan of metal. Her head snapped up and she saw the imp through a hole in the ceiling, crawling over the cab above her. She screamed again as his wet, bony hand slapped the thick, curved windscreen, leaving a filthy print in the dust. The croaking of the frogs was louder, all around her, a lustful roar. Her eyes squeezed shut as she drew in deep, ragged breaths.

"What do you want from me?!" she yelled. "Christ, what do you want?!"

The imp knocked on the front of the digger. *Chunk. Chunk. Chunk.* A signal.

"What do you want?!" she screamed.

Silence.

"Please..." she whimpered. "Please, please don't..."

Nothing.

Slowly, she opened her eyes.

The giant at the window had gone, but there were bloody imprints where he had pressed his gurning face to the glass. She looked up; the naked imp had dragged himself back into the reeds.

She was alone.

"Oh, Christ..." she whispered, laying a hand over her chest. Her heartbeat pounded and fluttered, and her ribs smacked her palm. *Chunkchunkchunk.*

She heard a single croak, somewhere beneath the beached digger.

"What—?"

Then the digger tipped forward. A shriek of rusted metal on metal as the whole thing pitched toward the water's surface, the bucket plunging into the pond as the ground beneath caved in and under. She moaned in agony as she was slammed into the dash, then clawed at the steering arch where the wheel had been, dragged herself up.

The windscreen was covered. Frogs crawled up from the pond—dozens, hundreds, thousands of them—smacking their webbed feet against the glass and batting their throbbing, yellow throats as they chirped and groaned. The weight of them on the front of the digger—Christ, streaming over it, stomping over each other, jumping from the bucket to the crane arm and then onto the glass with thick, wet smacks—was pulling it forward, dragging it into the mire, and all the while her window shrank, fat bodies writhing over each other and smothering the sunlight.

And in the last moment before everything went black, she saw him, standing waist-high in the water, sludge dripping off him in streams of grey and brown. His whole body was covered in a sluice of mucus-like pondwater, his skin a pale, deathly green. His smile was sickening, his head tipped to one side. He wore rags. They leapt around him, his amphibious minions, tiny bodies swarming the water at his waist, swimming toward her.

Then the digger tipped and the blackened window went smack and there was water everywhere and she couldn't see a damn thing, but she could feel the cold, the wet smashing inside, feel them everywhere, slimy bellies dragging across her face, slapping, webbed feet pressing all over her body.

Then the croaking was a thunderstorm, and the rain—everywhere, all at once—was enough to drown her.

Through bleary eyes, she saw shapes. Dark, flitting shapes in the red shadows of a firelit cavern, a cell of rough concrete and salt-crusted bars, streaks of blood and gold running down the walls. She smelled pondwater again and felt the heat from it rising to her face, thought for a moment she was still in that frigid water, still flailing. Then she tipped her head back and pain ripped through her skull, and she realized she sat on a stiff wooden stool, ankles and wrists screaming with pain; cable ties, pulled so tight her flesh was pinned to the bones beneath.

"Where...?" she moaned, but she knew where.

She didn't know how, or why, but she knew *where* they'd dragged her. Her eyes dropped and she found the source of the damp smell beneath her—a bowl of something grey and pulpy on the dirt floor, steam wafting up into her face.

Dinnertime, she thought, and almost broke into hysterics.

"It's awake," someone whispered. A child's voice. Whiny. "Can we start now?"

"Wait, Peach. Patience." A woman. Husky, almost a breath. "She must eat first."

She looked up and saw them. The grey-haired behemoth in the checked shirt stood behind the bars, and she noticed that the stitches in his lips had been replaced. In a shadowy corner of the room, the ghoulish figure from the woods stood scratching his crotch, shoulder jerking violently. He wore a pair of tattered dungarees, slung loosely across his otherwise-bare flesh. His clawing hand was stuffed into them.

Both of them were watching her hungrily.

And before her, a woman—was this the same one she'd heard out in the meadow?—sat on the floor with her hands folded, long, elegant fingers knotted together in prayer. Her eyes were closed. Her hair was cut close to the scalp and patchy, but she was strangely beautiful. A bruise-colored dress clung to her body, and where her arms and slim throat were exposed, they were bone-pale.

"You have questions," she said, eyes snapping open and flickering toward the bound woman.

She nodded. Her head slopped about on her shoulders. Had they drugged her? Christ, was she dying? Pain throbbed from her skull to her feet and back up again, and she couldn't tell which parts hurt the most.

She could smell burned metal, and tried to look into a square of bleeding light at one side that she thought might be a doorway, but only saw a mess of roots thrusting through a broken window, filling it, lit by a crooked lantern spraying them with gold like paint. The cell was in ruins. Fungus rippled across the edges of the ceiling, ribbons of yellow and gold.

Deep in the house, something croaked.

"Where am I?" she rasped.

"You're in our home."

"The things in the pond—"

"—the frogs—"

"—and that man..."

The woman smiled. "You are delirious. You were imagining him."

"You're lying."

"Yes."

Silence. Her heart screamed against the bars of its cage and her head pounded, blood thumping in her ears.

"I have kids," she said. "Please, they'll know something's happened. They'll know I came here—"

"And if they come looking for you, we shall let him have them."

Her blood ran cold. Stopped pounding. Stopped pumping. "No..."

"Pray they have more sense than their kin."

She swallowed. Thought about the figure in the pond. "Who was he?"

The woman sighed. "We—down, Peach—we call him the Master in the Water."

She looked, head swinging like a weight on a string. Peach—the foul thing from the woods—was halfway up the wall, scuttling like an insect, arms bent out, claws dug into the concrete. Drool hung from his mouth in thick, gluey strings.

"Who are you?"

The woman smiled thinly. "You can call me Mother. You've met Peach, and my husband, Malachi. Do forgive his rambling."

She cocked an eyebrow. Her head was sore.

"And this is my daughter, Messalina."

She noticed movement in the corner of her eye—over her shoulder, behind—and craned her neck to look. A girl sat on a stained mattress, ragged hair falling about a gaunt, pale face. She could only have been ten or eleven. It was difficult to say, because the girl's hands were in her eyes.

The bound woman frowned. No, the girl's hands were *really* in her eyes. Her fingers were gouged into two empty sockets, and thin trails of red gore ran across her palms.

"Is she a witch?" the bound woman asked.

"She would have been," Mother nodded, "many years ago. But no. She simply sees."

"How?"

Mother smiled as the woman in the chair turned back to face her. "He allows it."

"He?"

"Master."

The woman swallowed. "In the pond. I thought... I thought you'd left me to die there. With him." She remembered the frogs, crawling over the abandoned digger, over each other. "With them."

"Oh, we had," Mother blinked, as if stung by the obviousness of the woman's statement. "But he has other plans for you. You're not like the others."

"Others?"

"Food," Peach giggled. The woman looked up. He was on the ceiling, eyes wild and huge in his sunken face.

"What does he want with me?"

Mother sighed. "His body grows tired of him. He needs another."

"You're insane," she spat.

"Possibly. Anyway... Rest a while. Eat. Look, breakfast." Mother reached forward, nudging the bowl closer with a horrible scraping sound. "Eggs," she whispered.

The woman in the chair looked down. Grey goop swilled about in the shallow bowl. There was a lumpy texture to it.

No, the sludge *was* lumps. It was made up of hundreds of tiny, spherical sacs of translucent, mucus-like balls, all gathered in one gluey membrane.

Frogspawn, she realized, seeing tiny black dots inside each boiled, wet sphere. "Oh, Jesus..."

She kicked out. Her ankles were tied together, so both feet smashed into the bowl and sent it spinning, tipping out onto the floor. Above her, Peach howled.

Mother's face changed. "That was a gift," she said quietly. "Master is usually so...precious with his eggs. How dare you?"

Behind the bars, the giant—Malachi—moaned through his stitched-up lips. On the ceiling, Peach giggled like a child.

"Alright, that's enough," Mother said, standing suddenly, brushing the dust and shadows from her dress. She clapped her hands once. "Peach, take your father outside."

"Mother—"

"Now!" Mother snapped, eyes never leaving the bruised woman in the chair. "Out! Both of you!"

Skittering as Peach crawled toward the bars. The screaming sound of metal on metal. Shadows looming as the bars fell away and then swung in again.

Mother smiled down at her. "A little rest and some food would have made this all so much less painful for you," she said. "But since you're not hungry..."

"Let me go," the poacher said, "please, you don't need to do this. Let me—"

"Mess, take her to the cellar."

Hands clapped over her eyes—a little girl's hands, stained with blood—and she screamed as a thick, inky darkness flooded into her.

Air sucked into lungs. Stink of rotten tomatoes. Throbbing. Croaking.

Gasping awake.

"Shit!" she yelled, breathing fast, chest ragged.

Trying to move, to stand. Too weak. She flopped back down. Laid on the ground. Dusty floor. Sand?

Damp. Everywhere. And a shape...

His shape. The Master in the Water. Standing over her.

More croaks. All around. A voice: "Feed her."

Girl in her vision. Little girl. No eyes. Bloody holes in face. Hands red and screaming. Pouring, tipping something into her mouth.

Warm, wet slop. Lumpy. Sacs of mucus popping between teeth. Gagging. Vomiting. Pushed back down, *forced* back down by more of the putrid, spoiled stuff.

Black. Corners of eyes going dark. Protesting. Exhaustion. Pain.

Sleep.

When she woke again, she was curled up in the fetal position in the dirt, hands clasped beneath a cheek sticky with drool, one foot laid across the other. Her ribs and back ached, her mouth dry and acrid. She could smell sulfur and incense.

She blinked herself alert, looking around, easing herself up, groggy, disoriented.

She sat in a circle of white powder sprinkled in the dirt. Three rough, concentric rings, ripped into the shadows that spilled across the floor. The ground beneath her was bumpy, not pocked but rippling like a shallow dune. Looking out toward the cellar walls, she saw the floor at the edges dipped and fell away, swallowed by pools of thick, grey water. She was on a little island in the middle of it all, a moat of pond scum. Blossoms of frogspawn sprouted from the water, climbing the walls, knots and bundles of it running in upward trails like slick ivy plants.

There were frogs all around, their chirping a steady, low hum. They sat in the water, beady, black eyes glistening, tiny points of amber light reflecting and turning them demonic and malevolent. Some encroached the edge of her little island of silty sand, but none came within the first circle.

She was dry. Something had carried her here.

"He's coming now," came a soft, female voice from the corner of the cellar.

She craned her neck, wincing at the agony that pulsed through the tendons in her tight, bunched muscles, and saw the little girl from before sat on a low writing desk, its legs half-submerged in the water at the edge of the room. Messalina.

A wire shelf beneath the desk sagged in the middle; pinpricks of light dashed the darkness of the little alcove in pairs. Eyes looking out. More frogs sat on the table itself, and one—a fat, spiny brown thing—rested in Messalina's cupped hands, its bloated, yellow girth bulging between her fingers.

She was staring without eyes. "I see what he sees," said the girl. "I see the kitchen. He moves slowly. He'll be here soon though. The way to the cellar is through the door beneath the stairs. He's in the hallway now."

"Please," she begged. Her voice was hoarse. She wondered how long she'd been out. Hours? Days? "Please, don't—"

"Crawlspace," the girl whispered.

The woman frowned. "I don't under—"

"Shh..." Messalina said. "He's he-ere..."

The woman turned. Her eyes moved over crooked shelves framed in crude ironwork bracketed to the walls. Candles blazed, jammed into the sockets of little, polished skulls. Wax dribbled over grinning jaws and dripped over the edges of the shelves into the softly lapping water beneath.

Arcane symbols were scratched into the concrete, half-obscured by strings of twitching, bubbling frogspawn. The croaking was unbearable, and the rubbery creatures were everywhere, crawling over each other, bobbing in the water, climbing with long, stretched back limbs over abandoned chairs and tables, legs broken and sharp. Wide mouths in blank, black-eyed faces. Pulsing bellies struck through with pale, green veins.

A door screamed open.

She turned her head toward the sound and saw it. A square, crude hole in the wall, water swilling at its mouth, barely at knee height, if that at all. Darkness beyond.

Where did it go? Was this the crawlspace? Was the girl trying to help her?

Her eyes flitted up to the door, and she saw him.

Master was tall and slender, his hands hanging past his knees. His clothes were the remnants of black robes, eaten and worn by inclement years—decades? Centuries?—so that they clung to his narrow figure in rags. His legs were exposed, and the skin was the same sickly, pale green as the frogs' bellies, and run through with the same veins, patchy and mottled yellow inside his thighs. His arms were the same, though they were covered with brown, blotchy horns and stubs like the back of the toad in Messalina's lap.

His face was a mask of death. His expression was blank—the vacant, uninterested look of a frog—but it was pallid and tight against a bald, slick skull. His entire body was coated in mucus and flecks of seaweed.

He said, "I won't hurt you," and she almost believed him.

His voice was a dry croak, as if he hadn't spoken in years. When he stepped into the room, his feet—toes webbed, veins bulging against the skin—splashed softly in the water. His fingers twitched at his knees.

He said, "Do you believe in God?" and for a moment she

did.

"That isn't what you are," she whispered.

He smiled, his mouth spreading wider rather than turning upward. His throat bulged with every breath. At his feet, the frogs and toads grew excited, their own bodies pulsing with a sickening, almost lustful kind of admiration for the man in the sodden clothes.

"I am a god to them," he said.

She didn't know if he meant the frogs or the family. She wondered where Mother had gone. Had she simply left Messalina to take care of this?

"I have given them such gifts," Master continued, speaking slowly, softly. Carefully, as though each word were an effort. "Longer lives. More illustrious lives. Kept them fed, kept their bellies, their crops...moist. I live peacefully in the pond, and I eat when I am given food."

"This is sick," she said. "This is all sick—"

"Let Master speak," Messalina hissed behind her.

Master's smile fell. "Ah, the prophet," he whispered. "I have grown fond of the child."

"What did you do to her?"

"Allowed her to see. To see through my eyes, and yours... To bestow both sight and darkness upon others. A touch of the child's hands, and you might see all the secrets of the universe... or be blinded forever."

"And what about the others? What do they get for...for worshipping you?"

"They get to live," Master said, and he stepped forward.

The door swung shut behind him as the water swallowed his ankles. He glided toward her, raising a hand. He waved it a little.

All at once, the candles flared around her, and orange light erupted across the ceiling. She looked up, saw more symbols carved into the concrete—three concentric rings, mirroring the ones beneath her, so that she felt trapped in some invisible beam, and symbols that looked like spliced letters and digits, like twisted figure-eights and scrawled, mad numbers. A spell, an incantation...

A ritual.

The Master in the Water stood over her and showed her the back of his hand. She saw that the flesh was beginning to peel. "You understand," he whispered. "It will only be for a few years. And then your body will decay too, and I will free you and inhabit another."

She whimpered. This wasn't happening. None of it. Christ, her kids...

A dull chant began to resound through the cellar. Not human voices... The frogs. There were no words, but their croaking had risen in volume, each so individually mangled and distorted that, together, they formed a single, low hum.

"Please..."

"You understand," said Master, and it was like he wanted her to, like he *needed* it. "Don't you?"

"Please!" she begged, as the candlelight soared.

She couldn't move, frozen to the spot by fear. Above her, sick, green shadows trickled through the indents and patterns in the ceiling. The water all around bubbled and boiled. Master bent forward—

A pink shape leapt onto his back and clamped its hands over his eyes.

Her breath hitched in her throat as she saw black ink spread across the slender, green creature's face and then sink back into the sockets of his skull. He scrambled and clawed at the girl clinging to his back, but she held tight, looking up at the woman in the white circle and yelling, screaming furiously, "Crawlspace*! Now!*"

She bolted, the agonized wail of the Master in the Water echoing about the drowned cellar like an air-raid siren as he sunk to his knees, clawing and scratching at his face. Water splashed her face as she plunged into the shallow pool at the wall's edge and scrambled for the crawlspace, ignoring the plops and whistles of the creatures all around her. Frogs and toads leapt onto her back and legs, sucking at her skin with their rubbery mouths as they clamped tiny, webbed feet to her flesh.

She wriggled through the hole, not daring to look back or hesitate, diving headfirst into a tunnel barely wide enough for her shoulders to scrape through. Behind her, she heard the young girl shriek. Something hit a wall and went *thwump,* and then she heard Master roaring, bellowing so loud that the tunnel shook.

She crawled forward, splashing madly through water that rose higher and higher, freezing her chest and then slicing at her neck. Full dark, nothing to guide her but the downward slope of the tunnel, and she could only hope that it wouldn't go down far enough that she ended up completely underwater.

There was a crash behind her and rubble showered her feet as Master plunged into the tunnel.

"I can still smell you!" he screamed, and she looked back over her shoulder, saw pale green hands slamming and clawing at the walls, dragging him forward. His slender bulk blotted out the light from the candlelit cellar, and she saw black rivers running like tar from his eyes, eyes which had exploded in his face and sprayed his discolored flesh with ichor.

Kicking out at frogs that thrashed and bounced madly in the water around her, she crawled, straining her arms to keep her head above the surface, crying out as thick arms of pondweed caught around her and drew her back against the swell.

More symbols in the walls, these lit by a light from... above?

She looked up. A hole, a tiny pinprick of light, thirty feet above her. Rough, stone walls leading up. And rungs. A rusted, iron ladder embedded in the rock.

Freedom.

A hand wrapped around her ankle as she reached up to grab for the lowest rung. She screamed, kicking madly at the thick, heavy fingers, cold against her skin and so slippery and wet. The Master in the Water moaned as she smashed his knuckles into the tunnel wall and yanked her leg free, spitting water as she grabbed ladder and pulled, hauling herself up, up, up to the top rung. Exhaustion crackled like burning wood in her chest.

She swore. The ladder stopped. Still a long way to climb. She couldn't. She looked down, saw Master climbing after her.

No...

For your kids, she thought desperately. *Do it for them. Keep going!*

Digging her fingers into the stone, she clawed madly and hauled herself higher, scrambling for the light at the top of the well, heaving her wracked body up. As she climbed, it narrowed, the walls caving in so that her shoulder blades were scraped raw by the stone behind her and she had to push with her feet to climb. She felt her fingernails chipping and splintering, felt warm welts begin at her fingertips, heard Master smashing his way up the well beneath her—

"You're coming with me," he whispered, his voice more like the strained chirrup of a frog than anything human, and she felt his face brush her heel.

"Bullshit I am!" she yelled, and kicked down, hard.

Teeth clamped down on her ankle and she screamed, wet heat exploding from the ruptured flesh. She slipped, dropped, clinging to the wall with one hand while the other batted at the mad creature below, beating wildly at his face. Chunks tore from her heel.

And then he fell. In the half-light from above, she saw his face contort in surprise, saw his rags flutter as he crumpled into the water beneath with a splash.

Then they were upon him, thousands of them, bloated, brown-green bodies swarming his flailing figure until all she could see was a rippling mass of black.

"Come on!" she yelled, clawing her way up, adrenaline pushing her higher, faster, until her fingers dug for more flint and curled around the lip of the well.

She heaved, wrenching her body out through the ragged opening, tearing strips from her skin on the sharp stone.

And then she was free.

She collapsed in the wild grass, laying for a moment with a brittle fog of sunlight cascading over her. Free. The cool air brushed her face, and she remembered daylight as though it had been years since she'd last felt it.

Relief flooded her body and she laughed, punching her fists into the ground and scrambling up onto her knees. She'd made it, out of that awful house, that candlelit cesspit, away from the Master in the Water and the backwards family who...

No... The family...

Slowly, fearfully, she looked up.

Peach grinned down at her, his yellow teeth sprayed across blood-red gums. He had lost the dungarees and abandoned the shotgun, but he gripped the axe in both hands like he'd never held anything more precious.

"You're on private property, lady," he hissed, and then he shrieked with laughter and raised the axe high above his head.

WATCHING

By Selah Janel

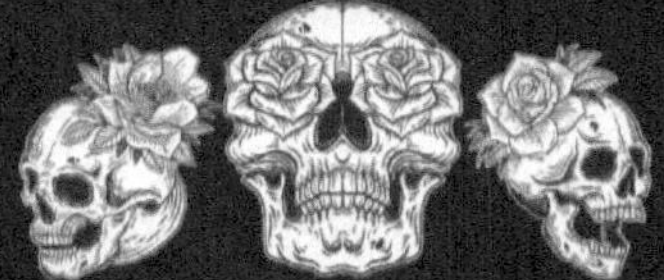

The voices always nudged John awake. They were pained, elusive, the voices of people he thought he'd known once but couldn't remember now. Any other time, he'd have thought it was the screech of an owl, or bad brakes on a country road. Spring was settling in though; that much was certain.

John felt the sound in his bones more than he heard it. His bleary eyes snapped open and, for a moment, he was alone in the universe, the weight of the nighttime overwhelming before his life, his place, his task took precedence. He rubbed a callused hand over his weathered face and checked the time on his phone. Black letters covered the rest of the display, bold against the glare of sudden, painful light.

IT IS TIME.

He blinked, fought the nausea, and looked again.

DO NOT BE LATE.

John fought the sigh and slid out from under the warm covers into the cool air of the bedroom. Angie slumbered on the other side, oblivious. The one night the Real World was awake, and her insomnia chose not to rouse her. He resisted tugging the aging quilt up over her bare shoulder.

Too risky to wake her, he reminded himself.

Not once in the years he'd been called to the ritual had she caught him, and he wasn't brave enough to see what would happen if she did.

Everything had to be done silently now that he was awake. It was more than his duty. It was tradition. The screams were too painful to be just a dream, the unease that wrenched him awake too much to be just a feeling. The dreams, and that specific sensation of yearning, only came when it was time.

The call changed with modern progress, but it always found him. When his watch, wall clock, and now his phone told him to go, he went. Just once he'd tried to ignore it. It had been his very first time on his own, when he was still a young man back on the farm, fresh from school after his father died— the old man's land now his responsibility.

He'd learned to take it seriously after that night.

The ritual was never quite at the exact same time of night, or even the same day of the year. He'd rolled over, tried to go back to sleep, too comfortable, too cynical about whispered backwoods traditions now that he'd graduated from college. He didn't care about the dreams that had told him what was coming, what he *had* to do. He'd tried to ignore it.

The nightmares had been immediate and horrific, sucking him into a dark, dark world that was more real than the world he lived in, even if it was inside his head.

The phone woke him, and desperate to be saved from the nightmares, he'd answered. The raspy, unearthly voice on the other end was something he'd never forget. It knew things no one had any business knowing, and he didn't doubt the future it predicted would happen if he didn't take his father's place.

He'd jumped right out of bed and never ignored it again.

Hell, I'm probably still alive because it was my first time and most things are forgivable once, he thought, with a yawn.

Now, older and wiser, John slid on the striped robe Bobby had given him for Father's Day ten years ago and a pair of old, no-name sneakers. He padded silently down the stairs, mindful of Pixie curled up in a black crescent on the sofa. The cat never woke on these nights, though, like Angie, she was a light sleeper any other time. It was the same for the rest of his family, as if whatever bound him kept everyone who was uninvolved under a heavy blanket.

John's reedy frame slipped out the back door. He walked the path from the yard down to the trees like his father had done, and his father, and on and on. He was fairly certain they'd all been called John as well. It was a traditional name for those who upheld the family customs.

Someone had to witness, even if they did not take part in the spring ritual themselves. It was better to have separate people involved, all with their own task. Tradition dictated that each family in the village was accountable, a member from each family all burdened by the need and the knowledge.

Either his Bobby or Craig would have to know soon enough. He wouldn't get to choose. One of them would simply wake up one year and follow him out the door. He hoped it wouldn't be soon. He'd hoped, by not naming either of them John, maybe they'd escape it. Every year, he kept his ears tuned for the faint pad of footsteps behind him, the dread that sound would bring greater than the one he already felt.

The night was a different kind of darkness than on any other night of the year. There was no moon, no stars, no other fields or houses. The only things that existed, that pushed hard against the suffocating blackness were him, the flat stones under his feet, and the silhouettes of trees down the way.

Maybe I'd stop existing if I stepped off the path.

It was a tempting thought. He'd learned not to look down, not to stare too much off to the side, not to look straight into the night. It wasn't that he saw anything per say, but he knew it was there, waiting for him to lose his nerve, to run, to back out of things. It wanted any chance to hunt, to shred his soul, and that possibility kept him moving forward.

Was such a ritual archaic in the modern day of internet

and cars and lattes and memes and things? Of course. His sons would laugh, if they even looked up from their phones. They wouldn't believe him if one of them wasn't compelled to. It wasn't time for them to know how the Real World worked yet.

John often wondered if those not involved—the ones that didn't flash a knowing look at the post office or the supermarket as the weather grew warmer—had any inkling.

He hoped so and he hoped not.

He came to the giant cluster of trees that was mostly ignored due to blight, though no one ever urged him to have the orchard put to a new use. He'd never offered. It was easy to overlook the specific tree in a small world of ugly, stout trunks and useless, scraggly limbs. It would have been unnoticeable, save for its size and place of honor in the middle of the orchard.

The body already hung from it.

The tree itself was gnarled and ancient, black branches thrust skyward into the night like the arms of the desperate. He'd felt like that tree so much in his life, yet this terrible, wonderful night had always made it better. He tried to think of the tree and not the corpse lashed to it. It was gruesome, there was no way round it, but the tree had to be fed. It was the oldest story in that part of the county, dating back well before there were counties.

Feed the tree and all will be well. Give death to the dead tree and your life will be blessed.

Thick of branch, deep of root, the thing's bark was gashed with ridges from countless spring rituals. Blood flowed down them like thin waterfalls in the light from John's phone. He tried to feel something deeper about the sacrifice, but he'd learned to wall off those thoughts years ago. The bark glistened the proper shade of red, still sticky in the damp night air. As John watched, delicate leaves sprouted, a good sign that the offering would be accepted. It was proof he didn't want, but grudgingly accepted.

Feed well, old one, and give us well in return, he thought.

Silence was part of things as well. He was there to watch, nothing more. A strange flash of pride and dark glee trilled through him.

What would the people in all those cars on the highway do if they knew what they sped past every day? What would the state officials say if they knew why the county prospered in a dead-end state? What would all those urban snobs do if given the choice to suffer or prosper? Would they have the stomach for it, like me an' all the others do? Not likely.

The pride helped dampen the disgust.

John chanced a glance down at his phone display. The commands had disappeared. The clock read three in the morning. Wasn't that the devil's time?

Devil ain't got nothin' on our tree.

He shuddered and pulled his robe tight about his torso before looking around.

Only darkness stared back. No grass, no house on the hill behind him. The other trees had melted into the void. It would be him and the ritual tree until the dawn, waiting with each other, watching each other as the darkness watched them to make sure it was done. He sighed and resigned himself to his duty, glad his bladder was calm for once.

He looked away from the darkness and back to the tree. He could never look elsewhere too long without feeling like he was becoming a little less human and part of some other universe that lay waiting.

Besides, the tableau was beautiful. Macabre, but poignant. Life was fleeting, but life continued in the tree. Death took them all, and death was also in the tree. The corpse's limbs splayed like graceful flower stems, head drooped, the body nestled into the branches like a lover embraced. He couldn't tell if it was male or female, friend or stranger. He always braced himself and was always relieved. He'd rather not know.

Wonder if Mary Hendricks put it up there. She has a knack for it.

He grimaced at the thought of her capable florist hands working each limb and finger, setting each just so with rope instead of floral wire. Likely she had help. It wasn't like they all met for coffee afterward like in church.

Still, sometimes he'd see someone out and about and know that look they had about them. He presumed he had the same look. He'd watched for it in the mirror until his face started lining with age, and then he found he didn't want to watch for it anymore.

Time didn't pass until it did, so it gave his mind plenty of chances to wander into treacherous alleys.

Where did you come from? Did they drug you in the diner? Were you willing? Who delivered the fatal blow?

It took all kinds, though he'd never taken the time to wonder where their offerings came from, if they'd had lives, who they had been before. He didn't live in a tourist town, and after the bypass had come, there were less people willing to wander through on road trips.

What happens on the day people stop coming through and we have to turn to our own?

John redirected his attention to the winding cloth decorated with prayers, requests and lamentations wrapped around the body, obscuring the face, chest and bits that the young didn't need to be looking at. Every full moon, he scrawled something he and his own needed and left it under a stone far out in the yard. Somehow, every time the ritual came around, everything he'd begged for was on the burial cloth, written in a strange script with blood.

He didn't recognize the handwriting. The other prayers were always illegible to him.

It's for the best. Not my place to know what my neighbors want. Let the darkness and the leaves read the desperate greedy pleas. As long as me and mine are seen to, what do I care?

Still, he wondered if others always got what they asked for like he did. Did Frank Sutton's cancer claim him because no one asked for him to be cured? Did Jerry and Kenna Beckman's shop go under because they hadn't believed enough? Was it dumb luck that he'd recovered from that car wreck just fine when he wasn't supposed to walk again?

He couldn't prove that it didn't work. All the logic in the world didn't explain the prayers on the cloth, the dreams, the disappearance of life until the sun came, the fact that, by time it did come, the body would be gone, though he never saw it move or disappear. Even though he watched, he couldn't say what became of it.

Why does it have to be this way?

It was a sudden, treasonous thought he would never, ever voice. He couldn't quite make up his mind if he believed or doubted, but he'd been at it so long he knew better than to back out. He was tied to this, tied to the community, tied to the tree, and if all he had to do was watch the body until dawn came to make sure it was good and dead, then he could do it.

It was an easy request for what he got in return.

At least I didn't have to watch the poor fool get killed. Or help.

There were other families for that. His owned the land— no one could own the tree—so his family watched.

The growing leaves danced, though there was no wind. The unnatural gesture was unsettling. John fidgeted with his phone but didn't look because he had to watch. It was part of the bargain, and if he didn't watch, he might not get what he needed. Or worse, the land might fail, or his children might die, or Angie might get sick.

This is the way it has to be or else the things in the Real, True World will get us. Someone has to feed the woods and the things in the night, or what's left of them.

He admired the blood to pass the time. The body looked like it had been young and strong. 'Comely', as they said back in the day. A worthy sacrifice. It would be a good year.

He shifted his weight, tried to ignore the fact that his

bladder was wide awake and demanding now, because he didn't dare defile the ground. Somewhere in the darkness, something moved, pressed closer, watched him as he watched the body. He took a step closer to the tree, swallowed against a dry mouth.

A finger twitched.

John froze. *It's a trick of the moon. The breeze.*

A hand spasmed.

He couldn't leave because he had to see it done, but he had never had to do anything but watch. He didn't even have a branch or a club to finish the poor soul off.

It won't come to that. You've done your part.

His eyes scanned the play of stagnant shadow over the planes and curves of soft skin.

"It's a trick of the moon," he reassured himself, though of course there was no moon.

He flushed hot at the realization he'd spoken aloud, then chased it with a cold wave of guilt for putting that much fear into superstition. Odd things were true, but he was a grown man, after all, and his family had always been faithful. Mostly. He'd kept up his end, even if he liked it less and less as the years passed, even if he found less and less to take pride in.

It was tradition. Necessity.

The head lifted as much as it could, face still obscured. The body sagged in its cradle after it gave a slight, exhausted tug.

"Please..."

The voice was ragged, almost extinguished. It was familiar. That realization nearly made John drop to his knees, though he couldn't place it.

It's one of us. It's finally happened. I could leave. It'll still end the same. Another ten minutes, an hour, no one will know. It'll still be dead come sunrise and I could come back out like nothing's happened.

But he had to watch. Every moment had to be accounted for.

John glanced around, dread puddling in his stomach.

Why can't we just live our lives without worrying everything'll be ripped away? Why our town and not somewhere else?

Those thoughts made him as sick as this whole business.

"Please, help me..." the voice pleaded, the mouth barely moving under the cloth binding. It trailed off on a small hitch of a sob, and John could just make out a quiver through the shoulders.

Helpless was not something he'd ever felt in front of an offering. Powerful, relieved, grateful, hopeful, disgusted, guilty, but helpless? It wasn't right or fair.

"Please help? Scared."

It was the voice of a child, of a timid, senile elder who'd lost their way, of someone vulnerable and just down the road. One of them.

Does everyone sound like this in the end?

He wanted to hear more, wanted to run from the terrible sound, wanted to make it stop so he could get back to watching.

"Hush now. It'll be over soon."

Surely whatever was out there couldn't fault him for talking when this had never happened before.

"Dad?" Tears slid under the prayers, mingled with crimson, streaked trails over the pale skin. "Dad, why?"

He recoiled with a curse, then launched himself at the tree. "Craigie? Craig, you weren't supposed to go out. Not 'til I say! What the hell were you doing?"

How had he not recognized his youngest? The scar on his hip from falling down the stairs when he was six was visible! He grabbed his boy's legs, fighting white-hot anger and mortification. The body didn't budge when he pulled. Craig gasped, and the leaves rattled in warning. John let go and leaned his face against his youngest, suddenly very empty, and so tired of it all.

"I can't. Son, I'm not supposed to..."

This isn't supposed to happen! I'm just supposed to watch it be done!

Something shifted in the darkness, slithered on the edges of his awareness. John could *feel* the dark growl rather than hear it.

"I can't..." he whispered.

His phone vibrated in his robe pocket. His face came away from the young man's legs, smeared with blood.

SEE IT DONE. THERE ARE OTHERS THAT COULD BE CHOSEN. NO ONE SAID IT HAS TO BE ONLY ONE.

John's stomach clenched and his knees fought to keep him upright. It would be too easy for something to happen to Bobby or Angie, or the whole town. As he stared at the text on his phone, another came through.

YOU ARE GIVEN WHAT YOU DESERVE.

"I can't save you," he whispered. "I'm not allowed."

He hadn't cried in years, but his eyes burned.

I'm selfish. I don't know how to save him.

"Why didn't you just listen?" he demanded. Anger was easier than the empty helplessness inside him.

Terror contorted the young face and his body went taut. "Dad, please! It's coming. It's... You have to..."

Again, Craig's lower lip quivered, and the words drifted off to something inaudible.

To hell with it.

Even if he couldn't save him, he could be with him and listen. Last words were important, and it was his boy. The dying saw things, learned things the living could only hope to hear and then forget. He'd never thought about what happened to the sacrifices' souls, but now the horror in his son's voice put a fear in him he couldn't describe.

He leaned in. "What was that, Craig? I'm right here, son. Talk to me! What can I do?"

His own voice was gruff, frightened, desperate. If the quiet had cracked before, his pleas well and truly broke through the nighttime spell now.

It broke other spells, as well.

Arms shot down before he could run. John thrashed—he was sure he did—but the willowy limbs were strong and unlike Craig. Brittle, twig-like fingers clenched his skull and pain ripped through him as he was drawn into the open embrace of the tree.

"Craig?" he gasped, eyes bulging, truly seeing now.

How he'd ever thought it was his son, he couldn't say. It was willowy where Craig was stocky, androgynous where Craig was masculine, inhuman where Craig was flesh and blood.

The thing's fair skin echoed the patterns of the bark, their strength the tree's strength. The wrapping of prayers fell away from the sacrifice's face, revealing a nightmare.

John screamed, his desperation turned to terror, but his voice barely existed. He tried to move, was sure he did move, but his body only twitched as it was drawn into the branches. The darkness poured over him, bound him further. The prayer-coated bindings slithered off the tree creature and wrapped and twined over John's body like a loving serpent. The less strong he felt, the more power shifted to the bloody words, the selfish demands of those he'd lived with for years.

He couldn't look away from the thing's eyes. They were dark, green and cold. Likewise, the sharp cheekbones, the long, spiked ears, the sharp teeth were far from anything he'd ever seen on television, online or in the fields.

"A lovely meal this time."

The thing looked him over like a curious child examining a toy it wasn't quite sure of. Its eyes sparkled and its lips pulled back from predator teeth. The thing's voice was thick and smug, and its breath smelled of fresh leaves and blood. It wasn't his son, but it was still recognizable. It had been many years since he'd heard it over the phone.

"No, no!" he whispered. Something inside him snapped. Staring into the face, feeling the press of the void, undid him from the inside out. "I did my duty. We watch—"

"You watch until it's time," the thing said, and nuzzled

his cheek with its own, inhaling deep, scenting him. "'Tis the agreement of ages old for me and my kin."

John's eyes felt like they would leave his sockets, the pressure in his head was so tight. "But you bless us—"

"What care we if we bestow a few trinket gifts in between, and use a few visions to get our way? What is it to us to make those we feed from believe what they will? 'Tis worth it to keep well-fed in this strange world."

"But the town—"

"Plays its part providing. Such lovely trees, and the things in them need to be fed, and one by one we pluck our fruit once it's ripe. Sometimes, the fruit is provided by the town, and sometimes the fruit is *of* the town. 'Tis a pleasing game we love to play." It cackled softly in John's ear, as if it was bestowing the most intimate of secrets. "This year, the others were bid to stay home, as you are the fruit to be plucked."

Terror and panic blanked his mind and prevented any reason from taking hold. "No. No, you lie!" he screamed, though the sound was muted in the grip of the thing.

If it's true, I've wasted all my life preparing to be fed to a... A...

He wouldn't name it, would rather think he'd been part of something bigger than been played for a fool.

"Such faith ye have and yet don't have. Ye mortals are exhausting. You've done your duty but pondered what is truly out in the universe. You'll have much time to ponder such mysteries."

It gave a sly, secret smile. Though he could only feel cold, John was aware of the thing embracing him, drawing him into the tree, into the Real World, where his soul would be set to wait as it was absorbed. His bones crunched, skin split and muscles contorted as he was taken deeper in. All that would be left was his blood, running down the gashes of the sacrifice tree to soak the ground and roots below.

If anyone came at dawn, he would be gone, the town's

latest mystery disappearance. He wouldn't get to warn his boys. The thing was cleverer than he'd ever been. It wouldn't be ignored, wouldn't be doubted, and believing would only end in more blood.

John knew it all, just as he knew he'd be trapped as part of this ancient, wild thing for as long as the tree existed.

The cracking of a twig sounded behind him, and for a brief moment, the thing paused in its feeding. John had lost the strength to fight, was so weak that he could barely keep his eyes open and his head upright. He didn't need to though, for the creature turned his head so his gaze was level with Craig's—the real, flesh-and-blood Craig he'd worked so hard to protect. This Craig was obviously still in the flush of youth, confident but tired, and confused as to why he'd felt compelled to wake up and take the path down to the orchard.

"You can't... Not him..." John wheezed, before his tongue stopped working.

"We thought you'd be happy that he was spared, such as it is."

The thing's voice brushed over him, was all around him, as he was sucked into the dark space of the tree. He bid Craig run with his eyes, but the teen stood there, shocked still, doing the watching that would be his job from then on.

"Now, now, you're ours now," the creature crooned, and John's head was turned back, the full weight of the tree, the thing, and the night a crushing presence on his body and soul as he was slowly, methodically devoured.

Until the creature was finished with him and John was no more, all he could do was stare into the wicked smile and glittering, steadfast eyes—

—and watch.

FERTILE GROUND

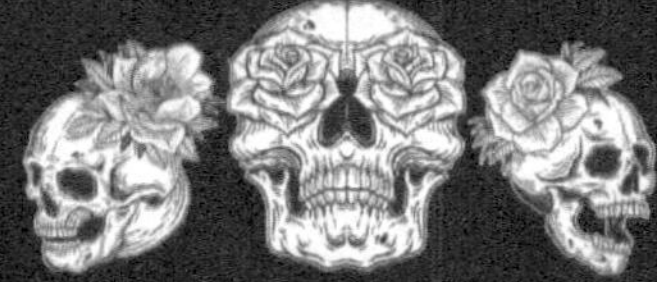

"Is there a word for something that's too beautiful to look at? So beautiful it hurts?"

Zella dangled her feet into the water below the dock. Across the lake, the reeds and cattails whispered secrets to the snow-capped mountains beyond.

"Yeah," Alice said through a smirk, "starts with a Z and ends with 'ella.'"

She kicked up a spray of water that soaked into Zella's linen dress before sprinting back up the dock toward the village with Zella hot on her heels.

A flock of Harlequin ducks, startled by Zella's cry, lit into the air and added their shrieks to the mix, their faces painted like masks. Her bare feet pounded against the dry-packed dirt, dress streaming behind her like a flag of surrender. The sweet smell of just-bloomed wildflowers filled her nose.

At the top of the path, Alice stood, hands in the air, chest heaving beneath her gray tunic with the effort of running uphill. "I give! I give!"

Zella barely slowed, planting her shoulder to Alice's middle and throwing both of them to the dusty ground, a tumbleweed of limbs and giggles.

"Zella Marie!" A shout cut through their revelry. "Right yourself this minute and go wash up. This is no way for a Legacy child to behave."

Zella pulled herself to her feet and brushed off her dress. "Apologies, Mrs. Blake," she responded, eyes to the ground, before darting a sideways glance at Alice who still sat, fuming, in the dirt. Zella silently willed her friend to stay quiet, but of course that never worked.

"We aren't children anymore. You can't just—"

"I can and I will, Alice. If you aren't children anymore, then stop behaving like you are. You know how important Zella is to this community, and I will not have you...corrupting her." She turned to Zella. "We feed the land..."

"So that we may be fed," Zella responded.

"You may be excused. Go make sure to have a healthy meal. You're expected at school tomorrow. This may be your final year, but you must still attend."

With one last, pleading glance at Alice, she turned and fled, the sounds of Mrs. Blake's reprimand tailing her like a wolf after a hare.

Her mother served her first, as usual. A huge, heaping platter of fresh-caught fish and fried duck breast and sauteed potatoes and kale. The carrot crop hadn't survived this year's late frost. Zella ate until her stomach was close to bursting, then her mother spooned on another portion. Zella's two younger sisters sat on the bench along the wall, eyeing Zella's plate with envy, the youngest, Ida, not even wiping the drool that pooled on her lower lip. They'd get some salted deer meat and potatoes once Zella finished. Her parents would eat last.

It was an uncomfortable affair, eating alone while her family watched. But her parents coaxed her on with nods and tense smiles, so she scooped more of the greasy meat onto her spoon and forced her teeth to chew. When her parents retreated to the kitchen, Zella often secreted dripping cuts of meat or flaky fish in a napkin to share with her sisters later. Ida and Violet would devour them, hidden under the back porch, letting the fats dribble down their tiny hands before licking each finger clean.

School opened on Mondays and Wednesdays. There, in the old, three-walled building that used to serve as a warming hut for intrepid mountain explorers, Mrs. Jansson taught history, botany, and sometimes reading. Mrs. MacIntosh used to teach reading and writing, but she was expecting, so she had been away from school for a few weeks.

"Fit to burst," as Zella's mother said.

Each student knew how to write their own names, and to read the labels on the garden plot signs. Some, like Alice, knew more and could read real books, but the elders told Zella Legacies didn't need to read, so Alice spent most evenings lying in the hammock behind Zella's cottage and reading to her from books borrowed from school. Sometimes pages were missing, torn out or rotted away with time and weather, and Alice would make up the stories to fill in the gaps while Zella stared at the tree branches overhead, always reaching for each other across the sky but never quite touching.

While the other kids sorted seeds, Mrs. Jansson drilled Zella relentlessly, mostly on history. The story of the first Legacy, born generations ago, on a night when lightning streaked the otherwise clear sky. The community had fallen into famine after a year of drought, but then the Legacy child was born. A child, according to the elders, who was prophesied to end their shortages.

From that time forward, the rainless lightning storm appeared generation after generation, gifting the community with Legacies and abundance.

Tuesdays, Thursdays and weekends were for gardens. Each community member had their own job, and Zella's was the blessing. She walked the rows of dirt and whispered blessings to the buried seeds. Zella knew it was an important job—the most important, in fact. The Legacies, born every fifteen years or so, were the reason her people survived, tucked away in their rocky mountain valley.

Yet, even knowing this, Zella snickered and squished up her face when Alice caught her eye as she walked the rows. Alice, covered in black dirt up to her elbows, dug potatoes out of a plot at the northern corner of the garden. In other, better years they had carrots and turnips and beets as well, but those beds lay dry and empty. Alice rolled her eyes and mimed Zella's slow, benevolent movements.

But Zella knew—when she thought she was unseen—that Alice dug frantically for hearty root vegetables that weren't there. That she woke early most days to trawl the lake for the fish that weren't swimming, that she wandered the empty woods searching for quail. When Mrs. Blake and the other elders complained what a lean spring this was turning out to be, Zella saw Alice's face grow tight, only to crack into a goofy smile the moment she noticed Zella looking.

For Zella's job extended beyond whispering blessings.

The day came, as Zella knew it would, when Alice pulled no potatoes from the ground, her father returned with no ducks, and the fishing nets returned empty. They still had their stores, but it would be a long winter if these meagre hauls continued. This was meant to be the start of the abundant season.

Zella strode the empty rows of dirt, chest held high, and lips moving silently through her benefactions. She held out her hands and touched each tiny, crumbling mound, willing sprouts to press through the topsoil. The elders would meet in the one room schoolhouse that evening, Zella knew, to whisper about rations and plans. In her lifetime, the food had never faltered, but she knew what it meant when it did.

Another gardener still knelt in his plot, though the others had gone home. He dug at the dirt erratically, sending chunks of it flying in all directions. The words he murmured reached Zella's ears as she neared. "We feed the land so that we may be fed. We feed the land... We feed the land."

Zella approached him, eyeing his gaunt face, his lost eyes. "Mister Patricks, shouldn't you go on home?"

He startled at her words. "You! Why are you letting this happen? We feed the land! We feed the land!"

Zella put a hand on his shoulder. "Mister Patricks, it will be okay."

His body stilled, hands deep in the dirt. He gazed up at her with his mud-flecked face, hope in his eyes, then stood and trundled off to the far side of the village.

On her way home, Alice ran behind her and slipped her mud-crusted hand into Zella's, squeezing tight.

"It will be okay," Zella said, inclining her head towards her friend's.

Alice's lips flattened into a thin line, her eyes glistening. She shook her head.

"Come on." Zella punched Alice's shoulder and took off at a sprint to the lake. "Catch me if you can!"

But Alice didn't run, just continued plodding, kicking up dust in her wake with each step.

At dinner that evening, Zella's plate was piled as high as usual. The sight of it turned her stomach, bile rising in her throat with each bite of salted fish and raspberry preserves. The noose had tightened. Her sisters and parents and probably Alice too would go hungry. Her parents watched like hawks, and Zella wasn't sure if it was because they imagined each scoop of food entering their own mouths, or if they wanted to make sure Zella didn't sneak any food to her sisters.

"Don't waste a morsel," her mother said, eyeing the plate with ravenous intensity.

That night, Zella dreamt the whole community stood atop her chest, pressing down, stealing her breath. But she knew if she moved, they would fall, so she remained still, gasping for air under the pressure. It was her fate, to be their foundation, lest they falter.

Her ribs cracked first, crushing down, then the other bones snapped and crackled throughout her body like dry sticks. The pain was immense, all consuming. The villagers knelt, pressing their mouths to her wherever they could gain purchase, ripping off chunks of skin and sinew. She didn't cry out. In her dream, she closed her eyes and whispered to the tiny seeds below ground as her flesh was torn from her bones.

She woke with a start, sheets damp with sweat. Outside

the window, in the quiet night, something flickered and flashed. Once, twice, and then darkness. Zella swallowed, trying to work saliva into her dry mouth. She crept across the floorboards, avoiding the creaky ones, and slipped out the back door into the night. The moon hung high, a fingernail crescent, shedding barely enough light to see the other cottages lined along the dirt path.

The hair on Zella's arms stood, electrified by the energy of the dark night. She held her breath. Streaks of silver lit across the sky, a zigzagging spiderweb cracking the black. A wail rose from the far side of the community. And Zella knew.

Mrs. MacIntosh's awaited baby had come at last, on the night of dry lightning.

An unfamiliar fear streaked through Zella, sending her back through the door on quicker, but no less quiet, feet than before. She slid under her blanket and pulled it to her chin, shivering, as another flash reflected off the walls of her room.

A new Legacy, arriving as her own abilities faltered.

It was time.

School was cancelled the next day so the community could welcome baby Harmony in the garden. Wrinkled pink cheeks, toes like tiny flower buds, fingers already clenched. Zella's heart thrummed at the sight of her, tucked into a wrap beneath Mrs. MacIntosh's beaming smile. But gazing upon the child coiled something inside her too, a snake poised to strike.

Alice flopped onto the blanket beside her, brown arms bare in the sunshine. She tried on her goofy smile, but even she couldn't fake it. Not today.

"When?" she asked.

"Tomorrow," Zella said quietly.

Alice's gaze wandered down the hill to the lake. She nibbled red trenches into her lip. "We could leave. Together. We could go somewhere far from here."

Zella gasped. Talk of leaving was blasphemy. "I can't betray them. It's my destiny"

"Oh, for the love of dirt, Zella! Will you listen to yourself?"

Zella shook her head, feeling suddenly dislodged, a dry leaf blown from a branch.

"You can't possibly want to stay, knowing…" Alice glanced around at the curious faces turned towards them. She lowered her voice. "…knowing what's going to happen tomorrow."

"We feed the land so that we may be fed," Zella repeated mechanically, but the coil inside her tightened.

She had a name for it now, not anger or resentment, but fear. It grew like a wild cucumber vine, twining around her ribs, strangling her lungs.

Alice must have noticed because she reached down to take one of Zella's shaking hands. "I'll stay, then. With you."

Zella exhaled. She turned her face up to the sun. "Do you think the plants know when it's time to meet their purpose?" she asked, eyes shut.

"Don't talk like that, Zell."

"Why?" She turned her gaze back on Alice. "It's a worthy cause. They feed and nourish us."

Alice opened her mouth to respond, but before she could, two sets of hands grasped Zella's arms and whisked her away.

"You've still to properly greet baby Harmony," her mother said, pulling her along.

"What a momentous day this must be for you, dear Zella," Mrs. Blake chimed in, from her other side. She released Zella's arm long enough to place a crown of woven reeds and wildflowers on her head.

"It is," she conceded, pulled along through the garden by the women's current to where baby Harmony held court in her mother's lap.

Harmony was asleep, yet community members whispered blessings to her and caressed her not-yet-chubby cheeks. As Zella approached, Harmony began to stir, tiny pink fists struggling out of her swaddle. Her mouth opened before her eyes, wide and searching. A hunger Zella never knew.

Mrs. MacIntosh shifted her wrap and offered her breast to Harmony. Zella had watched her younger sisters and other community members drink their mothers' milk, but still she marvelled at the simplicity of it. A closed circle: the mothers nurture and the children are fed.

But Harmony only drank a moment before she arched her back and howled, a shriek to rival a rabid fox. Murmurs passed through the crowd, and Mrs. MacIntosh's cheeks flushed. Her midwife, always nearby, stooped and tried to latch the baby again, but Harmony refused even more violently this time. Thick, white milk splashed off her cheek and down the front of Mrs. MacIntosh's dress. Her body tensed as the baby wailed again.

On impulse, Zella stepped forward. "May I hold her?"

Her mother let out a tsk, but Mrs. MacIntosh's face washed with relief as she handed the squirming bundle to Zella. The odd thought that Harmony resembled a freshly washed potato wrapped in a kitchen towel flitted through her mind. She arranged the baby in the crook of her elbow, as she'd seen the women do. Zella had never held a baby so small.

Harmony wriggled in Zella's arms, but the redness left her face and she quieted.

The assembled crowd fell silent, all eyes on the pair of Legacies. Zella felt her coiled wild cucumber vine ease ever so slightly. She exhaled.

"Hello, little Miss Harmony."

A tiny fist reached and twined itself around Zella's free finger. What a pair they were. Zella wanted to hate Harmony for displacing her. But instead, she felt an unexpected adoration for this child. She wished she could be like the apple tree, remaining tall and solid as it watched its fruit seed and grow anew.

But that wasn't the way of things. If Zella stayed, she would fester and rot like forgotten, fallen fruit. Fruit that would feed no one.

So said Mrs. Blake.

The next day was unseasonably warm. The sun painted the land in shades of honey, and Zella's new, starched dress chafed against her hot skin as her mother brushed and braided her hair. Alice came early, knocking on the door like a ravenous woodpecker before Zella's father had even roused and washed.

She rushed past Zella's mother with a quick, "Morning, Mrs. Oakes," as soon as the door opened and grabbed both of Zella's hands. "How are you?"

Her voice was low, strained, but she buzzed with energy.

Zella's mother hovered in the doorway.

"Could we have a moment, Ma?" Zella asked.

Mrs. Oakes lingered a heartbeat, then disappeared with a curt nod.

"Come for a walk with me," Alice said, not releasing Zella's hands.

"Alice..."

"You can. The ceremony doesn't begin until midday."

Zella's gaze drifted to the door her mother left through, then back to Alice's glistening eyes.

"Okay," she said, quietly. "Okay. Come on."

She led Alice through the main room, where her mother stood at the sink with soap up to her elbows.

"I'll be home in time for the ceremony," Zella said.

"You'll be home before that." Her mother's voice was gruff. "And keep your dress clean."

As they passed out onto the porch, Zella saw her mother wipe at her eyes with the edge of her apron. It sent a pang through her. The day suddenly became a real, solid, present thing, like finding spider mites on the squash leaves after seeing evidence of them for weeks. Her heart thudded behind her ribs as she stepped off her back porch.

Possibly for the last time, she realized.

Alice took the lead, heading away from the village and into the woods that bordered the lake and led up into the snow-capped mountains beyond.

"Where are we going?" Zella asked, conscious of the promise she'd made to keep her dress clean.

"Come on," Alice said, squeezing Zella's hand. Alice skipped on the tips of her toes, quick and eager. Sweat trickled down Zella's back, and her breath came in short bursts. "We're almost there."

They rounded a bend, and a small clearing opened off to one side of the trail. Some low-lying brush, ferns, two moss-covered boulders. And between them, a soft bundle, out of place. The bundle shifted slightly, the unexpected movement making Zella gasp.

Alice rushed forward and swooped the bundle up in her arms just as it began to keen. A natural noise, but so unnatural out here, alone, in the woods.

"Alice, what did you do?" Zella asked, her voice raising over the cries of the baby in Alice's arms.

Alice shifted her weight rhythmically from foot to foot, shushing baby Harmony. Her eyes met Zella's. Accusations, pleas, hope all muddled in their mossy brown depths.

"We have to leave. What they're planning for you today, for Harmony when she's older..." Her voice hitched. "It isn't right. They say it will make the crops grow, but Zella that just isn't true. It *can't* be true."

Anger flared, hot and painful, beneath Zella's skin. Her insides coiled, spiny blackberry thorns tangling through her ribs.

"How could you do this?" she asked, quiet. "You said you'd stay."

Her heart pounded against her thorn-tangled ribs, panic rising behind the anger. The earth tilted beneath her feet. *This isn't right.*

Her head swam.

Alice cradled Harmony closer to her chest as Zella took a step towards her. "Zell, I'm saving you. You and Harmony."

Zella could do nothing but shake her head. Her words strangled in the thicket that filled her middle, clogged her throat. A strained cry escaped her lips. Everything was crumbling. Everything she'd worked for. She remembered her dream—the villagers relying on her, their foundation. But she also remembered the rest: greedy mouths, tearing flesh.

And once again, she felt herself being pulled apart. Pulled by her duty to the village, by the love of her friend. She was being quartered, pieces of flesh, bones picked clean.

"Zell?"

Zella lunged forward and pried Alice's arms from baby Harmony. Her friend clung on, but Zella was stronger— months of healthy, protein-filled, meals while Alice starved. She pushed Alice back.

Harmony wailed, and Alice fell against one of the boulders with a dull thud. Zella's heart lurched, but she clutched Harmony to her chest and tore herself away with a cry of physical pain.

She darted down the hill toward the village, not allowing herself a backwards glance.

The air was thick with humidity by the time Zella reached the village square and gardens. Where baby Harmony lay against her chest, sweat and tears slicked the fabric between them. A crowd had gathered, like ants around fallen fruit, and cries echoed off the surrounding trees and houses.

Zella stopped a few paces outside the circle, her breath hitching in her throat, heartbeat thundering beneath baby Harmony. The crowd parted to reveal a distraught Mrs. McIntosh, her arms empty, face hollowed out and pale. She snapped her lips closed at the sight of Zella and Harmony. Silence hung in the air, electricity before a storm.

"What have you done?" Mrs. Blake's words clapped like thunder in the emptiness.

Zella shook her head, took an instinctive step backwards. "I— I didn't— I—"

"Silence!" the woman shouted. She came forward in quick steps and reached for baby Harmony.

Zella released the baby, as she knew she should, but felt the slice of a knife cutting away a piece of her.

Mrs. McIntosh let out a cry of relief, but Harmony's mouth opened wide in a howl. Zella's skin crawled.

Mrs. Blake turned her cold, steely gaze to Zella. "This community has grown you, tended you, nourished you, and this is how you repay us? This...betrayal?"

"I have betrayed no one," Zella responded, feeling herself teetering on a steep precipice. One step in the wrong direction, and she would fall into betrayal. "Harmony is here, and I am ready."

"I'm not sure it will still work," Mrs. Blake responded. A coldness spread through Zella, despite the heat of the day.

"Your heart needs to be nourished as well as your flesh. If your heart isn't behind this...then..."

Mrs. Blake spread her hands and shrugged.

"My heart is behind it! It wasn't me! I—" She cut herself off, visions of Alice crashing against the boulder swimming into her head. "*Please.*"

If she admitted it was Alice, she would betray her best friend. If she didn't, they'd think she betrayed the whole village.

Footsteps behind her, a commotion, an intrusion to the assembled group. Zella turned to find her father and Mr. Blake dragging Alice forward. Dirt caked the edges of her gray tunic and a stream of blood trailed from her gashed forehead down to her cheek and chin, where it hung like an overripe berry before dripping onto her collarbone. Zella's mother trailed behind, wringing her hands. She shot Zella an unreadable look.

Alice's face was taut, her eyes on the ground, jaw so tight a muscle twitched in her cheek. A simmering rage, hotter than the sun above. Zella's mouth hung open, words failing her.

Mrs. Blake stepped forward as the rest of the group took two steps back in unison, as though rehearsed. "What is this?"

Mrs. Oakes darted a glance toward Zella, then squared her shoulders and spoke. "She came to our home this morning. To see Zella." She glanced skyward and placed a hand on her heart. "They disappeared into the woods, and I— I had a premonition. I had Jerry follow them." She gestured to Zella's father, his thick hands still encircling Alice's bare, wiry arms. "She took Harmony. She tried to take Zella, but my Zella is loyal to this community. Not swayed by snakes hiding in the grass."

Her eyes fixed now on Alice, sharp with venom.

"No!" Zella cried out, unsure if she was disagreeing with her mother's account of events or her assertion that Zella was loyal.

Zella wasn't loyal. She was butchered, quartered, a million pieces of flesh.

"No," she said again.

Alice raised her head and faced Zella then, eyes pleading. She gave a tiny shake, as if willing Zella quiet, their roles now reversed. And Zella stepped into it without hesitation.

"No, Alice is innocent. The plan was my own."

She forced the words past her teeth and watched as each one hit Alice like a bullet. She shook her head at Zella again. But Zella couldn't let her friend take the blame for this, even if it was deserved. She had no idea what the punishment would be, but regardless, she knew it was something she couldn't bear.

The blood dripped from Alice's chin into the dry dirt in intermittent tap-tap-taps. Then she spoke. "Don't listen to her. I did it. I took Harmony. I tried to take Zella. To save them. You cannot raise your babies just to sacrifice them to the land. It's not right."

A susurration of uncertainty slipped through the crowd, heads swivelling from Alice to Zella and back.

Mr. Blake spoke from beside Alice as his hands tightened around her arm. "A Legacy would not betray us."

His words fell on the crowd like truth, as certain as the rains from the sky. A series of nods, heads bobbing like the reeds and cattails down by the lake. Zella's father caught her eye from Alice's other side, but his eyes were inscrutable.

"Charge her!" someone from the crowd yelled.

The cheer was picked up, repeated, chanted. "Charge her!"

Mrs. Wernicke moved from behind Mrs. McIntosh, her dirt-caked hands twisted into the fabric of her apron.

"Stop," she said, her voice gravelly. She cleared her throat and tried again. "Stop!" Her desperate, panicked eyes searched the assembled crowd for an ally.

Mr. Wernicke grabbed his wife, pulling her back with uneven steps, evidence of an old hunting injury. "Mae, enough," he said. "You'll get us all killed."

She wrenched out of his hands and stumbled toward Alice, but Mr. Patricks intercepted her. He pulled her away from the circle of people. She shrieked like a banshee all the while, until she cut off abruptly.

"By the vines," Mrs. Jansson whispered under her breath, quiet enough that only those closest to her could hear. She tucked a flash of sadness away from her face so quickly Zella thought perhaps only she noticed.

Mrs. Blake stepped forward, "Alice Wernicke, you are charged with kidnapping and disrupting the cycles of our society. How do you plead?"

"She's not guilty!" Zella cried.

Mrs. Blake turned an icy gaze to Zella. "That is not for you to decide, child. You've done enough."

"That's right, I have. I came back to you. I returned baby Harmony. I should have a say."

"Shush," Zella's mother intoned.

"I plead guilty." Alice's voice cut over the whispered crescendo of the crowd. Her face was moistened with wet tears. "I did it. I planned an escape for me and Zella. And baby Harmony. Because they don't deserve their fate."

That statement sent a niggling thought picking at the edges of Zella's mind, worrying at it the way she worried a hangnail. She *wanted* to deserve her fate, she realized. Alice couldn't strip this honor from her. *Why* didn't she deserve it?

She pulled the nail off and swallowed it, along with any more words she had to say in Alice's defense.

Mrs. Blake raised a hand, shushing the crowd. "This is an offense such as we've not seen in our community since its inception generations ago. Crop thievery, food hoarding, even murder." She paused and glanced around at the villagers. "These are all lesser offenses."

Nods of affirmation bounced around the square.

"An offense of this magnitude deserves an equally fit punishment." Her gaze landed on Alice again. "Alice Wernicke, in exchange for your attempt to disrupt the cycles of our society, you will now contribute to them. As retribution, you will conduct Zella's nourishment ceremony today."

"And if I don't?" Alice asked, chin high.

"Then your family will bear the pain that you've brought on this community."

Zella's knees went slack. The sun-drenched garden swam around her, dry dirt, crunching leaves, empty trenches. Her stomach heaved, and she swallowed to keep down the oversized breakfast her mother had served that morning.

Her mother. It was supposed to be her mother who wielded the knife during the ceremony.

Zella took a step toward Alice, but her mother held up a hand, her eyes shining. Stop.

Alice's face was all too readable though. An accusation rested there, blazing like too much sun off the surface of the lake.

A common shed squatted at the edge of the garden in the shade of a small copse of trees. Zella had never ventured inside, but when she was younger, she used to steal peeks through the windows at the shining hooks that dangled from the ceiling and the saws of various sizes hung on the wall. A smoker stood against one of the outer walls, and a fire ring a few paces away from that. A stone table was situated further out, between the shed and the potato patch. It shone white in the blazing sun, lying just outside the trees' shade.

Zella lay on the stone table, watching the buzz of activity from the corner of her eyes. She felt oddly distant, as though she were floating above rather than laying alongside the people of her village.

Mr. Blake and a few other men were finishing up the hole

between the potato patch and the carrots. Mrs. Blake flitted in and out of the shed like a worried robin, and occasionally Zella saw flashes of silver in her movements, glints of metal. Mrs. McIntosh, with Harmony now strapped securely to her chest, helped Zella's parents bring kindling for the fire pit and the smoker. The sweet, acrid scent of burning filled Zella's lungs.

Zella saw everyone. Except Alice.

Zella felt something move on her cheek and realized a tear slid from the creased corner of her eye down into her hair. Her insides tightened, strangled once again. If she had been floating above, as she'd imagined, now she would be falling back to earth with a bone-snapping crash. She suppressed a heave of her chest.

In a few moments, her throat would be cut on this very table, the blood collected in silver buckets to spread across the gardens. Then she would be hanged in the shed, drained like the deer her father caught in the woods, and sliced into pieces.

Another tear slid from the corner of her eye, but she forced the tightness away. She would nourish her community, as she was born to do. And the rest of her would be buried beneath the barren ground to give it new life. Her destiny, her honor.

Just then, Alice stepped out from the depths of the shed, Mrs. Blake at her side. Zella's mother approached and said something inaudible to Alice, who tensed and shot a glance towards the stone table. Nerves raced along Zella's limbs, and her heart pounded against her ribs like a fox in one of her father's traps.

Then they were there, beside her, Alice and Mrs. Blake. The woman handed the knife, which flashed like lightning, to Alice. She said something to the assembled crowd, but Zella's head swam, and the words rushed over her like a swarm of bees.

Mrs. Blake turned to Alice and gave a nod. Alice finally met Zella's gaze, a sparkle of sadness resting there. She gave her head a tiny shake and raised the knife. Zella squinted her eyes shut, readying for the blow. But none came.

Instead, a wet, metallic sound. A gasp from the crowd, followed by the splat of water against mud. Then a dull thud. And silence.

Zella opened her eyes to see Mrs. Blake's mouth hanging open. Everyone was frozen, as though time itself had stopped. Then things began moving all at once. Zella's mother rushed forward with a yelp; the villagers swarmed like ants.

Confusion and sunlight clouded Zella's vision. But then she saw Alice. Tunic stained red, body rumpled against the dusty ground, soiled knife still clutched in one hand.

"Alice!" Zella leapt off the table. "Alice!" She grasped her friend in her hands, but her arms were cold, limp. "What have you done?"

Zella's face was wet with tears, her heart sore, as though somehow bruised within her body.

"We must still finish the ceremony!" Mrs. Blake's words thundered over the din.

Her strong hand encircled Zella's wrist and pulled her toward the table. She'd already retrieved the knife and wielded it in her other hand.

"No." It was Zella's mother. She stepped in front of Mrs. Blake. "No. This has gone on long enough. Perhaps Alice—rest her soul—perhaps Alice was right."

The hitch in her mother's voice made a lump rise in Zella's own throat.

"That girl has nearly ruined things for this community," Mrs. Blake responded, through gritted teeth. "We need to feed the land."

"What we need is a good rain," Zella's father said.

"Exactly," Mrs. Blake insisted. "We must complete the ceremony. And the rains will come."

Zella watched, silent, as the villagers split like water around a rock. "We can feed the land with something else," said Mrs. McIntosh, from Zella's side. "Our children are neither food nor fertilizer."

"We must feed the land so that we may be fed." Mrs. Blake's voice rose an octave.

Others joined the chant. "Feed the land so we may be fed!"

A crack of thunder split the gathering. Zella's father held a gun in his hand, raised to the sky. "No one is touching my daughter. Now I suggest you all get home and have yourselves a dinner of whatever you can find. And give thanks for your family."

"Who gets the girl?" came a voice from one of the villagers, gesturing to Alice's body.

"The earth," Zella's father responded, low and steady. "We'll bury her—rest her soul." He wiped at his eyes. "This is what it had to come to, eh? I couldn't even speak up to save my own child. Another child had to do it. I'm thankful to her. Thankful she showed me the way."

He clapped a hand on Mr. Wernicke's shoulder. The man stood dumbstruck, staring at his daughter's broken form.

Zella's father stooped to pick up Alice's body. Numbly, Zella helped. She watched her friend be buried in the hole meant for her.

Summer raged hot and dry. Winds blew up dust cyclones across the barren gardens, and Zella grew thinner with each passing day. Gone were the days of feeding Zella first. Now, they all starved together. They ate whatever was left in their stores, then the berries and leaves. When fall came on, they chewed sticks.

Zella watched her village waste away to nothing and felt the weight of it on her as she had in her dream. It pressed her down, crushing her.

One morning, as the wind whipped through the leafless

trees beside their house, she found her mother too weak to rise from her bed. Zella searched the pantry for anything edible, but she knew it was futile.

Mrs. Blake's cottage was beside the school, small and austere, made of shorn tree trunks, like her own. Zella's knuckles cracked hollow against the door. The woman who emerged looked like a ghost of Mrs. Blake rather than the woman herself. Her cheeks pulled into hollow pockets, her posture hunched. At the sight of Zella, her eyes widened, but then quickly narrowed.

"What do you want?"

"I need you to do it, Mrs. Blake." Zella handed her the knife she'd retrieved from the garden shed. "You must. For the community."

"Who's it?" Mr. Blake's voice echoed from the shadows beyond.

"No one," Mrs. Blake said, but she stepped out with Zella and closed the door behind her.

The sky hung low with dark clouds as they walked the short path to the stone table. With no rain to wash it away, Zella could still see the faint stain of Alice's blood on the dry dirt. She lay back on the table, already feeling a lightness about her, the weight lifting.

The slice was swift and expert, and Zella felt the blood flow from her in a rush of ecstasy.

She heard it drip into the silver buckets with metallic pings, just as the first drops of rain touched her cheeks.

THE OLD MAN OF THE ROOKS

By Bryson Richard

The old man leaned stoically in a field sown with barley. He was alone, save for the rooks that circled above, floating casually on gusts of cool air with their midnight wings. There were hills behind him, where the wind formed the shapes of serpents slithering through the crop. A farmer tended to the barley way back among those hills.

A fencerow of trees picketed the landscape to the right of the old man, dividing the barley from a field of tall, yellowing corn. He had become accustomed to the trees, and imagined faces hidden in the gnarled bark and knotted limbs.

The sky above him was low and fast-moving. Heavy grey clouds, the color of lead, hovered seemingly just above the old man's head, and the rooks swooped in and out of the mist like salmon leaping from an inverted river.

He wore a floppy, wide-brimmed hat of straw that had seen much use and wear by someone else before he'd been gifted it. A long, colorless scarf, unraveling and half-eaten by insects, was coiled around his stick-thin shoulders. It was banded around by the wind, entangling in the old man's outstretched arms to flap franticly.

Sometimes, the rooks grasped his arms and shoulders with

their talons, and bowed under the old man's hat, as if whispering secrets. He was not bothered though. As with the trees, he was accustomed to the birds and knew each one intimately, to the point of tedium.

He was lonely in his silent observation of the countryside. He held himself in passive indifference though, maintained his position in the barley field and watched as the world changed around him. The leaves in the fencerow were enflamed a vibrant orange and deep red. They gradually let go of their branches and plummeted lazily to the ground. The days had grown shorter and cooler, the nights were longer and mischievously active.

He observed one of these mischievously active creatures now, entering the field. A young woman, Autumn. Her fingers tickled the thigh-high barley tips as she passed through their ranks. Long hair, as red as the fiery leaves still grasped by the trees, coiled around her limbs and torso like ivy. Her pale skin held the same eerie luminescence as the full moon on a clear, cloudless night.

She approached, and the old man saw her eyes were the same deep grey as the clouds suspended above them in fleeting wisps.

"Hello, old man," she breathed, "How are the rooks this day?"

"Always loyal, always close," the old man said.

She reached out and adjusted his hat to study his face. "Have you seen the mess the foxes made?" she asked, excitedly. "They killed a whole henhouse last night. Must have been two dozen hens in there, and naught but feathers left once the foxes were done."

The old man studied her, trying to decide if she were attempting humor.

"You should have been there," she muttered.

"I do not go anywhere," he said directly. "I stay where I am needed and useful, here in the barley field, with the rooks."

"And do you ever wish to do something different? Perhaps

you could be of more use elsewhere?"

She couldn't tell it, but the old man was frowning. He was bewildered by her—by her intrusion, yes, by her suggestions too, but also by his enjoyment of her presence.

"What brings you to my barley field?" he asked her.

"The season." She waved a hand, indicating the landscape around them. "It stirs a wanderlust within me. A desire for travel through fields and meadows, through forests and along country streams. Searching, always searching."

"What is it you search for?"

"Acolytes," she said simply. "Revelers in the falling leaves. Sycophants of the harvest who will journey with me to the patches where gourds grow." She shrugged, "Those who will visit the warm hearth of a shepherd's cottage or climb silver threads of moonbeams and converse through the firmament."

"Conversation?" the old man asked. "You seek companionship."

She laughed. "Indeed! Though I have plenty of worthy companions already, I might welcome one such as you," she jested, eyeing him warily.

"If only I could go. I would be a terrific companion."

She giggled, as if the suggestion was humorous, then stood back and looked him over. "What kind of companion would you make? You have no legs with which to roam with me, no hands with which to hold mine." She patted the old man's face. "Your skin is rough, and you have no mouth with which to laugh. And your eyes are only buttons! How could I gaze into lifeless buttons?"

The old man said nothing, but the rooks cawed above on his behalf. There was a gust of cold wind and the old man's scarf flickered, obscured his view, and when it settled, he saw Autumn running over the hills and into the trees.

The rooks fluttered around his head and chided him with caws, pecking at his hat and pulling his scarf taut around his neck. Their chastising went unchallenged by the old man, who stood motionless in the barley field.

At dusk, the wind died, and the moon, clear and supple, shone like a beacon over the silent field. The old man remained still all through the night, and the rooks were never far.

At dawn, as the sun glowed on the horizon in an aurora of gold fog that crept across the dew-wet barley, the old man spoke to the rooks.

"If you truly revere me, heed my call."

The rooks extended their bedewed wings to dry as they alighted on him, awaiting his command. He spoke to them in a whispering language, like the crisp rustle of leaves blown by the wind, offering instruction and direction.

When he finished, the birds crashed into the morning sky, an explosion of sooty wings and piercing caws. They passed through the air as a great, formless shadow, in tune, in tandem, then suddenly split and scattered to the horizon.

And the old man waited, as he always did. As he was made to do.

Far behind him, across the rolling hills and silhouetted against the rising sun, the farmer began his day, scythe in motion.

The first rook returned at midday. Two ripe eyeballs dangled from worm-like optic nerves clutched in its beak. They were plucked from an old tomcat that hunted the local fields and woods.

Two more arrived shortly after, carrying the dry, moss-stained mandible of a long-dead and forgotten hound.

In the early evening, several rooks appeared, hefting a pair of coveralls they'd lifted from a clothesline. The weight had caused them to drag the garment through field and wood, and it had become considerably soiled. The old man did not mind. All these things they found through his direction. All these things he saw in the open, rolling distances before him.

The rooks attended him, removing his button eyes, and replacing them with the cat's. They sat askew on his face, globs of gelatinous grey with dandelion yellow irises and black slit pupils, and stared out at the barley field dumbly, unblinking. They mounted the mandible to his head, where his mouth would be. Two sturdy hickory limbs acted as a skeletal structure for legs, and the coveralls were pulled over them and fastened at his thin shoulders.

Dark was near when the last of the rooks finished. The old man waited through the night, uncomfortable and uneasy with his new appearance.

The dawn lit up the edge of the world, brimming with enough rising light that he saw Autumn, far off along a distant tree line, approaching him as if summoned by his patience.

"What's happened to you?" she sniggered, when she was near enough to perceive him.

"I seek only to impress you, Lady," the old man said, the mandible moving awkwardly on his face. He'd never had a working jaw before.

"Well..." Autumn smiled and gestured at him. "You still have no hands for me to hold, nor feet to follow me. You never move, old man. You are inert. I am always in motion, always scurrying through forest, field, branch and brook. How will you ever keep up?"

She threw her arms into the air and skipped around the old man, startling the rooks, and sending them into an uproar. Their protests amused her.

A breeze blew through the barley, carrying orange and yellow leaves which spun and flowed around Autumn and then flared away. She chased after, forgetting all about the old man and his modest changes.

Before evening settled in, the old man again spoke to the rooks and again they flew to the horizon. They began to return by early morning. They fashioned a crude ribcage of twigs and vines over the old man's torso, and a pair of old sneakers, previously hanging by their laces over a telephone wire, were attached to the old man's hickory-limb legs.

He waited for Autumn's return all that day. Then all the next. And the rest of the week, and then the rest of the month.

Slowly, the farmer in the distance maintained his progress, inching ever closer to the old man in his toil.

As the month ended, the old man became aware of further changes taking place around him. More and more, the fleeting warmth of the afternoon was absent from the day, and the night seemed to stretch on indefinitely. The loneliness of the long, cold, howling winter awaited him, he knew, and even the rooks would depart him for a while.

One evening, as the last of the sunlight spilled out over the horizon, blinding the old man where he stood in the nearly barren field, he had another visitor.

Mr. Wintrus, bearded and bent over a gnarled wooden cane, came at his own plodding pace across the field. Mr. Wintrus was even older than the old man, and the two glared at each other with loathing.

Then Mr. Wintrus prodded the old man with his cane. "What have ye gone and done to ye'self?"

The old man didn't answer. He preferred not to engage with the ancient, white-bearded Mr. Wintrus, who's cruelty and contempt were well-known. Instead, the old man watched the horizon and hoped to see Autumn skipping over its rim.

"Ye look as if ye want to be something ye have no business being." Mr. Wintrus pressed on with his observation. "I can tell. Usually, it's Lady Vernal that gets them who live in field and forest lively, which is as it should be; the Lady is ever blooming, such is her reign. But the gloom of Autumn's entrapment surrounds ye. A fascination, I pity. She brings naught but decline and decay. She befriends the souls of night and together they sabbat around bonfires, reciting memories of the past. She will not be tamed, old man." Mr. Wintrus shook his head gravely.

"What would you know of it?" the old man huffed.

"I know enough. Yes, I know that those who surrender

to Autumn's dead leaves and night fires, wind gusts and gourd gardens, inevitably come to me. And you will find that I lack the warmth and whimsy of even one who admires the dark and decay such as her."

"Begone from me," the old man muttered.

Mr. Wintrus muttered back his own judgements and passed slowly from the field. The rooks dived and tugged at him as he went. He turned them back with a wave of his cane and they called after him in insult and ire, as most do who encounter Mr. Wintrus.

The days passed and Autumn did not visit. The old man kept a sagging cat's eye on the horizon. The rooks too searched, but even their soaring eyes could not detect her. The once ragingly beautiful trees were now sourly bald, furrowed and cowering in their starkness. A scattered few clutched bundles of candle-flame leaves in their crooked branches like outstretched hands. Autumn's reign was soon to end, and Mr. Wintrus would hold sway.

That evening, as the sun sat in an eruption of flaming oranges and pinks, and the farmer, ever-toiling, had nearly reached the old man in his bent march of harvest, reducing the field to a naked, cropped bareness, Autumn materialized in the napalm sunset, a silhouetted collection of tendrilled hair and curves.

The old man averted his dead cat's eyes, trying to ignore the agonizing infatuation that swelled within him.

"Hello, old man," Autumn said, and the noticeable absences of her usually frivolous and flighty attitude caught the old man by surprise.

There was a sincerity about her that he did not expect, a maturity, beautiful and terrible as an elder, old-growth forest, ablaze in the fiery hues of her reign.

"You're still here?" she said to his silence.

"I have waited and watched through night and day for you," the old man croaked. "I've had many visitors in my lingering watchfulness. I've heard whispers, claims of you seducing the lonely and despondent, stealing into their domiciles in the night through jarred windows and down drafty chimneys. Is it true that you coil around their hearts and seep into their very blood? Do you kiss their lips blue and lure them, moonstruck, through wood and meadow?"

"I am loved by exceptional few," Autumn said. "The lost, the forlorn, the poet and painter, those who live for long nights and frosty dawns. I visit each according to my whim and each embraces me as fully as I embrace them. I make no secret of this, old man."

"I've waited," the old man sighed. "Watched."

"And I've been frolicking in branches and across treetops, singing to the moon on cool, silver fountain nights, then skimming over babbling brooks in the early, misty morning, as is my right during my reign. What of it? What are days and nights to one such as you, ever-prone, ever-still, ever-present?"

"The moon?"

"As much a friend as you, old man, only we enjoy the added pleasure of nightly processions across the firmament."

The old man shivered but did not step away from his spot among the barley.

Autumn moved closer to him, and the rooks who rested on his shoulders and hat lifted their wings, but did not take flight, nor dare to utter a note of interruption.

"You wish to accompany my parade? To engage in the march of Autumn is a task for the quick and nocturnal. It is of the owl and the wolf and the black goat. You must follow my whimsy and keep up. Those reclusive few that I seduce march with us."

"Perhaps they could hoist me or—" the old man began, but Autumn cut him off.

"I am sister of Artemis and Hecate, cousin of Demeter, and her daughter, Persephone. To follow me is to follow the night, the harvest, to balance on the rim of decline, on the border of life and death. I am the delight of the decay. What makes you worthy? You, who never ventures forth, who remains, watchful, aware, but bitter as unripe apples. What makes you more worthy than this farmer, who labors in this field, carves his lanterns from my gourds, lights his bonfires in my honor, partakes in my ceremonies? What quality do you hold that he does not?"

The farmer, who toiled only a short distance from them, paused his work, looked around himself as if he'd heard a voice, wiped sweat from his brow, gazed out at the sunset briefly, then bent back to his labor, giving no notice of their presence.

"There are some who say you smash their lantern gourds," the old man said coldly. "They say you spread their bonfires to field and home and wood, uncontrolled, and loosen their livestock from fences and pens. Is that how you ingratiate your loyal disciples?"

"My domain is coupled with trickster, psychopomp, and sprite." Autumn flapped a dismissive hand. "A certain mischievous quality is eminent."

The old man narrowed his feline eyes and the rooks he commanded became agitated, lifting their wings, their caws sudden, sharp, accusatory.

"Mischievous quality?" the old man spoke. "I will show you the quality of the rooks."

The birds took flight in a screaming mass of infernal blackness. They surged upward, an apparition of feathered unity, and then descended like a wave on the startled farmer. The man thrashed and beat at the birds with his scythe. His screams were drowned out by the angry caw of the rooks who swarmed him, picking, plucking. He tried to flee, but the swarm directed his movements towards the old man, and suddenly they lifted him in a collection of frantically beating wings. The farmer's blood rained down on the small patch of unharvested barley that surrounded the old man, splashing the stalks and muddying the ground.

Swiftly, the oblong stick arms of the old man sprung out and pulled the screaming farmer out of the air, and the clamor of rooks entombed them in fluttering midnight.

Moments later, the rooks receded and revealed their labor.

The farmer lay at the old man's sneakers, a pile of steaming entrails and disjointed bones.

The old man flexed within his new skin, cat's eyes peering crookedly from the smeared, stretched remnants of the farmers face, the lower jaw sickeningly under-biting, jutting out at an angle. The jawbone did not fit under the flesh it wore. Stick fingers poked through the tips of the farmer's gloved hands.

The old man took a jerky, awkward step towards Autumn.

"Well, it's about time," she said, blessing the old man with a smile, before she turned and walked towards the fencerow. "We were beginning to think you'd never come, old man."

The old man moved his jaw in a way that he hoped made a smile and stepped away from his spot in the barley field after her.

And the rooks, flying low and predatory, followed them.

Night descended, and all of Autumn's acolytes emerged from their slumbering nests—nocturnal predators and their prey, wandering psychopomps and their eclectic friends, and the moon above, watching them gather and lighting their assembly with pale waves of luminescence.

The crests of dark hills in the distance sparked with sporadic fires that grew hungrily, and shapes and silhouettes gathered around the alluring beacons, glowing invitations for Autumn and her parade.

BROKEN HARVEST

By Michael Quay

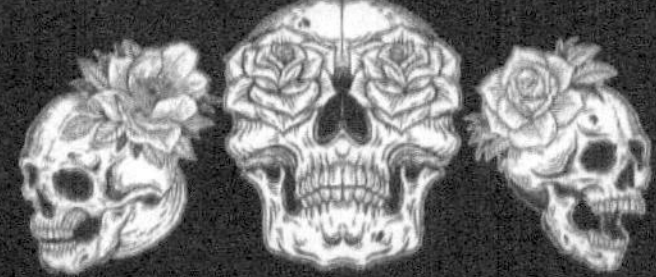

PROLOGUE

Regina stood at the bottom step of the small, white church in her nicest black dress. She leaned against the railing, staring out at the forever sky that blanketed the sea of tall grass across the road. The sun had already set, coating the field in a hue of gold. This had been her spot every Sunday growing up. Where she would wait for her father to leave church, to hold her hand in his, and lead her to the truck.

He was a hard man, whose life and toil were intertwined, especially after the death of her mother so many years ago. He had raised her like he did the crop; he worked tirelessly to follow the right steps, but the end result mainly depended on the weather. She always resented not being more than that to him.

But as she stood in this familiar spot, the hard bulge of the railing at her back, she felt a clarity. She understood him. Understood that what he put into those fields, and into raising her, weren't competing paths but rather a single thread, a summation of a man's life that amounted to what he had built around himself. Those fields were not instead of her; they were *for* her. Now she had to be for them.

He once promised that he would take care of her until the end. Today was that end. And the beginning of something else.

Colton emerged from the church. He cautiously approached Regina at the bottom of the steps, putting his hand on her shoulder.

"Ready?" he asked, with concern.

Regina stared off. "Not sure."

"I'll be in the car." She watched him slink towards the truck, head hanging low, his hands in his pockets. He looked odd wearing a suit.

The field of grass swayed softly across the road.

A silver box sat on the coffee table in the middle of the living room. Regina paced before it as Colton stood with arms folded. The darkness of night had emerged after the long day; they had been in that room for hours.

She stopped. "It's time."

Colton nodded.

She reached over and grabbed his hands, cradling them tightly in her own. "I need you to promise me something. I need you to promise me that you'll step in. This house, that land. It's ours now." Regina swelled with emotion.

"I married you, didn't I?"

"I mean it. Really promise. The way father wanted. No more drinkin'. No more messin' around. This is our life now, and we need to make this work. I need you." Tears began to roll down her face as she strained to keep her composure.

Colton locked his eyes with hers. "I promise."

"This is your life too. Don't say this on account of me."

He pressed his head to hers, feeling the wetness of her skin. "I promise."

Regina pulled away and softly nodded. She turned to the box on the table. "It's time then."

She picked it up and walked out of the living room into the neighboring kitchen, gliding towards the door at the back of the room. She swung it open, revealing the vastness of the farm outside. Stalks of corn filled her view as she moved down the dirt path, away from the house.

The night sky hung overhead, blanketing the crop with stars. The air was cold. Regina cut into a row of stalks as they swayed softly.

She slowly flipped open the lid of the box and poured the contents around her, coating the ground with powdery, gray ash.

Regina sank to the ground, lying her body flat and spreading her arms across the cold earth. Above her, the leaves of the stalks cut their outline into the night sky, which was coated with white specks like fallen crumbs.

She closed her eyes and breathed in deep, clutching the dirt between her fingers.

In the distance, Colton watched from the back window.

CHAPTER 1

The sun bled in deep, red currents, washing the heavens with dry, quivering air and dull heat, clouds streaked across the sky like paint.

Colton wiped beads of sweat from his forehead. His blue work shirt was soaked with a sharp streak that ran down his back. He had just walked out here. How was it so hot?

He lifted a shovel and stamped it into the ground. It clanged as dirt and dust kicked out of the puncture. The reverberation hurt his hands, but Colton repeated, driving the sharp tip of the shovel into the earth in articulated stabs.

Dammit.

He lost his grip and let go. The shovel bounced as it hit the ground. Colton looked at the inside of his hands, skin taut and red. He squatted down and traced his finger along the mark in the ground. Barely a dent.

He stood and looked around. Rows of corn crop struggled to stand, dried and brittle, wilting in the heat. He plucked an ear off the stem and unfolded the leaves like burned paper. Seeds like rotted teeth, loose and shaken, fell to the ground.

He dropped the rest into the dirt and looked back at his hole, his dent, the plot before him that needed the plow, but which wouldn't tame easily.

Somewhere in the distance, a bird cawed as it drifted through the thick daylight.

The old, compact tractor's engine rumbled to life. Colton steadily drove it forward and stopped, positioning the machine in front of his hole. He looked behind at the plow hitched to the back. Long ago, it had been painted a bright orange, but now it was dull and chipped.

He slowly pressed the gas and lowered the plow into the ground. The tractor stuttered forward, plow clanking loudly behind as the cut refused to burn through the hard terrain. It skittered through the dust before catching on something, pulling back with a metallic screech.

Colton felt the tug from behind. He brought the tractor to a stop and hopped off, engine still humming. He grabbed the plow with both hands and tried to shake it free, but it was wedged stuck.

He lay down, looking underneath. The knife of the plow had cut into the earth right at the spot of his shoveled hole but had caught behind a large rock. Colton grimaced as he reached, trying to dislodge it, pushing and slapping at it with his fingers. It didn't budge.

He marched around to the other side of tractor and picked up his discarded shovel. He walked back around and again laid on the ground, his stiff, blue shirt scraping against the crumbled rock.

The engine rattled as the sun beat down, heat colliding with the dry air in a meld of shimmering disturbance.

Colton tried to wedge the shovel under the rock. He swung his leg beneath for leverage and tried again, this time spearing the tip into the dirt. He inched it forward, the blade of the shovel sliding deeper. He steadied his leg against the wheel and pushed hard.

The shovel speared down, bouncing the rock violently upward where it hit the bottom of the plow, shifting the wheels out of their original position. The momentum of his effort sent him to the ground, belly-first, his leg exposed.

Freed from the hold of the rock, the tractor lurched forward, dragging the plow with it.

Colton felt a searing burn as the knife sliced through his

leg, lodging into the fabric of his jeans and tearing through flesh on its way to bone. He felt himself being pulled as the plow dragged his body across the ground.

His eyes lifted towards the sky, blinded by a flood of white light, the engine of the plow roaring. His hands lunged behind him, flailing, pulling only dust and stone, face dragged across earth now fresh with the red smear of his blood.

With all his might, Colton rolled his body away from the moving plow, his momentum strong enough to dislodge his leg from the grip of the knife. His body flipped, landing hard on the ground with a thud. The tractor continued, the back tire of the plow rolling up the side of his belly and down the other as if he was a mound of dirt, crushing the air from his lungs.

Colton gasped. His eyes flooded with a mixture of sweat and tears. He could make out the tractor and plow cutting their path forward, leaving a streak of blood along the way. His leg was a pulsing mixture of burning and numbness, the ground around him soaked red.

He tore at his shirt, ripping through the buttons and yanking his arms out of the sleeves. He found the deepest cut on his leg and tied it around, tight as he could. The pain was overwhelming. He tried to yell her name.

"Regina...!"

Weakness overtook him. His body splayed on the ground, the saturated white sky pressing in from above, the roar of the tractor engine slowly fading as it continued to roll forward. The sun blared without mercy. Colton closed his eyes and sank into the dust.

CHAPTER 2

Regina's eyes shot open. Frantic, searching, breathing heavy, heart racing. The textured ceiling, some kind of off-white cream. Her head was spinning. She focused on the peeling paint near the corner of the room. She tried to find her place.

She sat up, straining to catch her breath. A bad dream. Always these bad dreams. She tousled her black, curly hair, trying to rub the reality back in as she kicked her legs over the side of the bed.

The wisp of the sheer curtain danced before the open window, evening light cutting through the fabric and scattering onto the floor. The air was still hot and dry from the day, but the evening had started to take hold.

Downstairs in the kitchen, Regina washed her hands. It was time to cook dinner, and while she knew there wasn't much in there, she opened the refrigerator door anyway. Wishful thinking maybe. A jug of milk. A loaf of bread. She might make lentils tonight. An onion, some leftover broth. Simple.

They were struggling. Struggling with the bills, to fill their lives with the comfort of a security that she *knew* they could have. This farm used to give her that. She knew it could bring that to Colton too, if they were only able to make it happen. After her father passed, it was on them to make it work. Fair or not, she knew most of that fell on him. But it was one thing after another getting in their way. The drought sure didn't help.

Where was Colton? He should have been back by now.

She looked out the window. Somewhere was the faint hum of a tractor engine. Somewhere far.

The sun barely peered over the distant horizon, cut by a line of trees miles away. Evening was setting in. The corn crop stood brown and wilted, kindling in the dirt. Nothing moved.

Silence, save for that faint hum of a distant tractor.

She pushed open the back door and stepped outside.

The air was dry and crisp, but Regina was struck by how alive it felt, like an approaching storm was about to show itself.

There, in the distance, she saw it. A glimmer of light attached to a plume of exhaust. The tractor. She focused her eyes, locked on the string of smoke withering in the distance as her feet kicked up dust walking towards it. She nearly went right past him.

"Colton!"

He was sprawled on the ground, skin drained of color and left an unnatural pale. He didn't look real.

Regina grabbed his head, cold and wet. Her eyes searched up and down his body, trying to understand what had happened. His clothes were soaked in blood, deep brown and stiff, the ground around him painted the color of his insides. His lips, cracked from the sun, tried to whisper but couldn't muster the strength.

Far off in the distance, the engine of the tractor hummed as it continued towards oblivion.

CHAPTER 3

Colton stood in the middle of the church, flanked on both sides by rows of empty pews, wooden beams crossing the high ceiling like a web. Regina, wearing her nicest black dress, knelt before an open casket.

He took a step forward. He began to extend his hand out to her but stopped. The casket was empty.

"It's not going to be easy. You know this."

Colton turned around. Sitting in the front row was Lee, Regina's father. He was wearing a crisp, black suit with a red bolo tie. His head was lowered, the wide brim of his black rancher hat concealing his face.

"Lee?" Colton tried to speak but found only a whisper.

Lee's hands were clasped in his lap, wrinkled and weathered, skin clinging to bone.

"She's yours now. I can't anymore." As Lee spoke, his head rose just enough to reveal his mouth, open gaps between rotted teeth.

"He doesn't want it."

Colton shot around to find Regina with her back turned towards him still, kneeling before the casket.

Lee coughed out a chuckle. "What he wants is... immaterial."

He lifted his head. Beneath the hat, his face was dark, the sun-carved crags outlined by shadow, eyes hollow like pits.

His chuckle turned into full-throated laughter, which reverberated through the room. Coughs began to emerge, violent and deep, intensifying. Blood spattered on the tile floor, droplets turning into streaks. Teeth shot from his mouth, catching in the forming puddles.

Colton took a step back. He spun around to Regina, who

remained in front of the casket. Her head began to shake with a frenzied vibration, back and forth, shoulders contorting in an angular hunch.

He reached out his hand and touched her shoulder.

Colton woke with a gasp. He shot up on the bed and collected himself.

His leg throbbed with pain. He peered under the blanket to find it wrapped in a large bandage, still white and clean.

"Regina!" he called out.

Nothing.

He pushed himself out of bed and wobbled towards the door. He used the railing to slide down the stairs, dragging his feet behind. His leg ached. Ached bad.

In the kitchen, Regina was washing dishes, the clanging of pots too loud to hear his call. Colton lurched to the table and sat down.

"What's for dinner?" he called out.

Regina jumped, startled. "Colton! Why didn't you call me?"

He smiled. "You must not have heard me."

She gently put her hand on his shoulder. "How are you feeling?"

"I'll be alright." He paused. "I need to finish the crop."

"Colton..." Regina looked at him with concern.

Colton stood up and shuffled towards the door. "We miss another harvest, we're going to be in bad. We could lose everything."

He turned towards the door and leaned against the frame, looking out the window. His eyes widened and he looked back at Regina in shock.

"What is it?" she asked.

Colton pushed the door open and shuffled outside. The corn crop, which before had been a collection of wilting husks, was now lush green.

"I don't understand..." Colton mumbled as he lurched forward, moving as fast as he could.

Regina stood at the door, confused.

Colton burst into the rows of stalks, green and alive. He grabbed an ear and twisted, tearing it off the stem. He looked up at Regina, who was still trying to process what she was seeing, and laughed.

He tore open the leaves. His huge smile dissipated, turning into a kind of bemusement.

He held up the ear of corn. The kernels were bright red.

"You ever seen this before?"

CHAPTER 4

The sun hung like a burned hole in the cloudless sky, red and throbbing, blanketing the earth under its weight.

Colton slammed a crate filled with ears of corn into the back of the old pick-up truck, sliding it into place amongst the others already stacked in the bed. Every inch was filled. He threw a tarp over the top and tied it down.

Regina watched by the porch steps, leaning against the railing.

"You going to be okay?" she asked.

"I'm good," he mumbled. He took a beat. "We got no choice, Regina."

"What you think they're going to say?"

Colton shook his head as he limped to the front of the truck. "We'll find out."

He hopped in and started the engine. The truck puttered to life and slowly rolled onto the road, Colton's hand extending out the window with a wave goodbye.

Regina watched the truck disappear down the road, the back of the tarp flapping in the wind.

Kernels dropped into a bowl as Regina scraped an ear of corn with a knife. She picked one up and studied it. It had a dark, red center that permeated outwards in lighter gradients towards the tip, which was more pink.

She popped it into her mouth. Not bad. Slightly sweet. The aftertaste was odd, more savory than crisp. It gave way to a slight metallic taste. She dumped the rest into a pot of boiling water on the stove.

Colton drove the truck towards a hand-painted, wooden sign: FARMER'S MARKET.

Despite the size of the lot, there were only three tables set up, one of them in the process of being taken down. Colton recognized the man packing up as Royce, a farmer from the other side of town, who he ran into regularly. He pulled over and hopped out of the truck.

Colton raised his hand. "Royce! Good morning!"

Royce looked up. He was older than Colton, his skin dark and cracked. His eyes were weary, red with exhaustion. He stood up and stretched his back.

"Morning, Colton. You selling today?"

Colton looked around at the near-empty lot. "Anyone buying?"

Royce shook his head. "There's nothin' here. This heat, I'm telling you. Not a drop in the sky. Just...somethin' in the air, and it hasn't been good." He turned back towards his things. "I don't know how any of us are going to make it through the season."

Colton nodded. "Keith here?"

Royce looked up. "What you want with Keith?"

"Just want to talk to him. He around?"

"Yeah, Keith *was* here. He's probably three in at Pullman's. You got something for him?"

"Couple drops I squeezed from a stone." Colton limped towards the truck. "Thanks, Royce."

"What happened to your leg?" Royce shouted.

Colton raised his hand, but continued without stopping.

"Plow accident."

Royce watched as he hopped into the truck and peeled off.

BING. The kitchen timer went off.

Regina removed the dish from the oven, placing it on a wire rack to cool. The baked corn casserole was normal in appearance, save for the reddish tint.

She placed a large helping on a plate and sat down at the kitchen table.

She eyed the food suspiciously, then picked up a spoonful and shoveled some in her mouth.

Regina loved this casserole recipe. Her mother would make it often, a creamy, sweet dish almost like a pudding, but substantial enough to be a meal. Unfortunately, it was not something she'd been able to make much lately, the crop being what it was.

She chewed slowly. It tasted...good. Really good. It was sweeter than normal, with that additional savory touch. She took another mouthful. It wasn't *just* as good; it was better. The creaminess slid through her mouth, her tastebuds swirling.

Regina kept eating until her plate was empty. Her head began to spiral. She darted to the counter and brought the entire dish back to the kitchen table. Her body flooded with warmth and her toes curled as she ate. Her veins pulsed and her head flushed. The feeling enveloped her. Regina's eyes rolled back in her head as she swallowed mouthfuls.

She buried her face in the dish.

Colton knew Pullman's well, but it had been a while. As he entered the bar, everything about the place hit him at once. That smell, like damp sawdust. The buzz of grunts and laughter, the low hum of a jukebox somewhere in the background.

Keith sat at the bar, his cowboy hat on the counter next to his whiskey neat, his red hair and mustache caked with sweat and dirt. He worked for the wholesale company that bought produce in bulk from local farmers. He was also a drunk.

Colton slapped his back. "Keith, is it lunchtime yet?"

"It is somewhere, Colton." Keith took a sip from his glass. "Didn't see you today."

"How was it out there?"

"Dead. Just dead." Keith shook his head. "Not sure how we're going to handle this."

Colton smiled. "Let me show you something."

Regina slumped backwards in her chair, eyes closed. Her mouth hung open, smeared with red residue. Her heavy breathing pushed its way to the surface through scratched gurgles.

Her eyes suddenly shot open, bloodshot. She picked up the glass dish and licked the insides, smearing her face against it.

Cleaned off, she slammed it back down and moved towards the door. She darted outside.

Colton threw the tarp off the bed of the pickup, unveiling the stack of crates.

Keith's eyes opened wide. "What do we have here?"

"Picked yesterday."

Keith turned to him. "How did you get all this?"

Colton smiled. "Family secret."

"May I?" Keith reached towards one of the crates.

"Now, Keith, there's something you should know..." Colton started.

Keith didn't hesitate, however, and tore into one of the ears.

"What's this?" He held up the corn; plump and healthy, perfect even. But red.

"This, uh, farming technique to harvest in this kind of weather, but..."

"It's not some pesticide is it?" Keith interrupted, not interested in an explanation.

"Of course not." Colton grabbed the ear and took a bite. "Try yourself."

Keith shrugged and took a bite. He looked at Colton as he chewed.

"I'll take it all."

"Well... Jesus, okay!" Colton could barely contain his excitement.

"Let's get this in my truck." Keith smiled as the two shook hands. "Then, let me buy you a drink."

Regina crouched on the ground, staring at the oven, eye level. She breathed fast and heavy, lungs pumping, eyes feral, red with bloodshot.

BING. The kitchen timer.

She sprang up and yanked open the oven door. Inside were five different casserole dishes. She pulled them out and dropped them on the counter.

Keith and Colton stumbled out of Pullman's. They slapped each other goodbye, and Colton watched as Keith headed back inside.

Colton ambled towards his truck. He looked at the empty bed, beaming. He hopped in and started the engine, then took a deep breath and pulled out of the parking lot.

The truck made its way down the back country road, slowly drifting to the side and then correcting itself back to the center. Drifting again, and then correcting. Colton shook his head, trying to stay focused and awake.

He saw the stop sign. It was right up ahead, where stop signs usually are. He eased his foot off the gas and moved it over to the brake. He felt its outline. Then he went blank.

The pickup truck shot through the stop, easing just slightly but not nearly enough.

Coming up the road was a black sedan. A flash of blue as the truck cannoned out from the side road and barreled into it.

The impact sent the car spinning, the front folding in like paper. Metal twisted as it spun in a circle like a leaf in a drain. The momentum carried it off the road, past the shoulder, through the grass, which elevated into a hill. The angle sent the car up into the air and onto the other side.

Both vehicles lay, unmoving, in wounded heaps.

Colton's eyes fluttered open. He wasn't sure where he was.

He faced an open field, which he could see through the badly cracked windshield. He was behind the wheel of his truck. His head throbbed.

He stumbled out and collapsed to his knees. The violence of tire tracks left scars on the road in all directions. Colton could smell the burn, metal and glass scattered across the pavement.

At the peak of the hill, adjacent to the road, lay a tire. The grass leading up to it was torn apart into clean mud like it had been cut by a plow.

What was left of the black car was crumpled and torn, like a rolled-up newspaper left out in the rain. Colton could see a man in the driver's seat. The airbag had deployed and was pressing against his body, enveloping his head.

He cautiously limped towards the car, moving in slow motion as if he was waist deep in water. Every step hurt, his head throbbing so hard he could barely see.

Colton pulled the door open.

The body of the driver appeared headless behind the airbag, his limp appendages hanging like old clothes. Colton shook his shoulder.

"Hey! Hey! Are you okay? Hey!"

Colton panicked. He had no idea what happened, and no idea what to do. Adrenaline had cut through his drunken haze but that was turning into a stew of weary delirium. He wanted to collapse.

He pushed in the airbag and pulled on the body, exposing the face of the driver. He was young. Colton felt near his mouth; he was still breathing.

He yanked off the seatbelt and pulled the driver onto the grass by the car. His face was badly bruised, blood spewing from a gash on his forehead. His arms and legs looked intact but were limp. He was unconscious.

Colton knew he was drunk. He also knew that if he left this guy out here he'd die. The car had shot high enough over the hill that it would be easy to miss on this side road, barely travelled to begin with. He didn't have a phone. The nearest hospital was an hour away. He had to get him help. Regina would know what to do.

He wrapped his arms under the driver's armpits and pulled him through the grass, legs dragging like the train of a wedding dress. When they reached the road on the other side of the hill, Colton set the man down and went across to get his truck.

The front was caved in, splintered with shards of black paint from the car. He hopped in and started the engine. It stuttered but came alive. As he backed up, he could feel some kind of misalignment in the axle, but the old pickup was moving.

The stranger had not moved. Slowly, carefully, Colton hoisted him into the passenger seat. He affixed his seatbelt, and closed the door. He limped his way to the driver's side as fast as he could. Colton looked at the man, slumped against the door. He took a deep breath and eased the battered truck forward in a stuttered lurch that smoothed out over the open road.

CHAPTER 5

The truck screeched to a halt next to the house. The front door was wide open, the curtains lazily dancing in the breeze. Colton nearly fell out of the truck.

He screamed. "Regina! Regina!"

The man had pressed himself against the side window, the gash on his head spewing blood across the glass like a popped water balloon.

"Regina!"

Colton opened the car door slowly. He mustered all his strength to hoist the man onto his back, carefully balancing him on his shoulders. He moved as fast as he could, hunched over, like trying to carry a bag full of water before it fell and broke open.

His boot hit the first step of the porch. Colton clutched the railing, face pale and drenched with sweat. He raised his other foot, straining to keep balance. He could feel the strength draining from his body. He was going to pass out.

"Regina!" he called again.

The curtains on the door frame drifted leisurely in the breeze, the light from the early evening casting an orange glow across the texture of the white lace. They lifted like the two extended arms of a ghost, beckoning him into the darkness.

Colton wanted to sleep more than he'd wanted to do anything in his life. His head wasn't throbbing as much as it was collapsing in on itself. He closed his eyes, took a deep breath, and pushed. He pushed so hard.

His boot lifted and dropped onto that last step. He was on the porch, legs wobbling as he shuffled towards the door like a newborn calf. The curtains outstretched, pulling him forward, welcoming him in.

Colton could feel his legs failing him. He pushed inside the house, propelling himself forward and flung the unconscious man towards the sofa. Down he went, landing softly on the cushions, while Colton landed hard on the floor.

He slid himself over to the side table next to the sofa and willed his arm to rise like he was working a marionette, gliding it to the phone that sat on the glass table. He picked up the receiver and pressed 9-1-1. He heard the phone ring in his ear. Then again.

CLICK.

Dial tone.

Colton looked up in astonishment. Regina stood over the phone, her dark hair hanging like Spanish moss from a tree. Her hand rested on the switch.

"Regina?"

She stood silent.

"Regina? We need to call an ambulance! We need help!"

She shook her head wildly, hair whipping, as if to pull herself back into the present. Her skin was so pale it was almost translucent, with what looked like pink veins winding through her face. Her eyes were bloodshot.

She pulled him into the chair next to the couch where he sunk down, his strength crumbling into the cushions. "You smell like booze."

Colton broke. "Yep." He nodded. "Yep. You're right, Regina. I hit him. With the truck. I don't know what happened. I think I… I must have…" He began sobbing as he struggled to speak. "I did this. I did this. I don't know if he's okay. I don't know."

"You're drunk," Regina snarled.

Colton looked at his feet. "We have to help him."

Regina studied the stranger. "This doesn't look good."

She grabbed a towel from the kitchen and pressed it against the gash on his head. The moment it touched his skin, the man's eyes shot open, frantically scanning the room.

"Colton, get up!" Regina barked.

The man pushed to his feet, balance shaky. As he stood, blood poured down his head and hit the rug in a spatter of crimson that soaked into the fibers.

"Colton!"

He felt like he was barely there, his legs and arms numb, his head swimming. He somehow dragged himself to his feet, where he swayed in place.

The two men struggled to keep themselves upright like battered boxers, Colton wobbling while the stranger clutched his knees.

"We're not going to hurt you, friend." Regina took a step forward, her arm extended. "Now sit down!"

His eyes locked on her. He pushed himself upright, his entire body leaning as if it was about to tip over.

"Friend, just sit down. You need help!" Regina took another step, her words more forceful.

The man let out a grunt as he swung himself to the side, using his momentum to hurl his body into the kitchen.

Regina watched but didn't move. She turned to Colton. He stood in a daze, his eyes closed, body swaying. She put her hand on his shoulder and stepped in close. She whispered into his ear like an incantation, steady and without pause.

"He's going to get the police. What do you think they're going to do when they get here? They're going to put you in handcuffs. They're going to take you to jail. You murdered that man, Colton. Look at his head. Look at the floor. Colton, look at the floor!"

She gripped his shoulder tightly.

Colton's eyes opened. He could hear loud rummaging and soft groaning from the kitchen as the man worked his way through the room. On the beige rug below him was a spattering of red, flung and felled in all directions. It was everywhere, like a painting.

"He's already dead, Colton. Don't let him tear us apart.

Don't let him destroy us. You're letting him get away, Colton. You're letting him destroy us."

Colton's eyes widened; his breathing intensified. He could see flashes of movement in the kitchen. The watery pool of his brain swirled, picking up speed as the entire room spun around him, save for the stable eye of the kitchen doorway.

"Colton, save us. Save us. Protect us. You promised. He's already dead. He's already dead."

Colton took a step towards the kitchen. Then another. He watched his boots hit the floor as he moved closer to the doorway. He pushed and swung himself into the kitchen to see the back door slam shut, the stranger gone.

"Colton!" Regina screamed. "Get him, Colton! Get him!"

Colton moved as if shot with adrenaline, everything pumping at once. All he could see was light.

He slammed into the door and crashed outside, somehow maintaining his balance as his feet continued to move, boots hitting dry dirt, pushing, pushing.

He saw the stranger ahead, stumbling into the rows of corn. A trail of blood poured from his head and diffused into the dirt.

Regina followed. "Get him! Get him!"

Colton pushed. Closer. Closer. Dust everywhere.

The stranger turned around. Blood streamed down his face, covering everything but his eyes, which were wild with confusion and fear. The man opened his mouth and let out an unmistakable word that was barely a whisper, his last forced breath: "Help!"

Colton leapt, cutting through the air as the heat of the sun pressed against his face. He crashed into the man, sending them both to the ground. The stranger groaned as Colton found his hands circling his neck.

"He's going to kill you, Colton!" Regina screamed. She was right behind them. "He's going to kill us both!"

Colton felt the thrust of her words like she was digging

her fingers into the back of his skull and pinning his eyes to the ground. He clenched his hands as hard as he could, the rough skin between his palms tightening. He closed his eyes.

He could see the corn, ready to be picked, green and plump. That smell in the air as the stalks were cut, the fresh hint of dampness, like a salve from the heat. The thin leaves that tore, not like paper but like skin, like peeling dried glue from your fingertips as a child, the eyes of a watchful mother that caught your own between the halting moments of her own thoughts, the promise that you would always be cared for, always together, never alone, and as you become that unto yourself and those worries passed forward, those fears, that hole of utter blackness that was chasing him down and pulling him in, that pit of nothing that he vowed he would never face alone again.

Colton felt his grip loosen. He opened his eyes. Before him lay not a man but a heap, the assembled remnants of something no longer as it once was.

He sat up, hands red and wet pressed on his blue jeans. He struggled to catch his breath.

Regina put her hand on his shoulder. "You did the right thing, Colton."

He looked up at her, his eyes heavy. Her black hair hung in clumps, face smeared white, veins crawling everywhere just beneath the skin. Her stained eyes were wild, a wheeze in her breath. She looked like a demon.

"I killed him," Colton whispered.

"He was already dead when you brought him in the door."

Colton shook his head. He rose to his feet.

"This ain't right, Regina." He turned towards the house. "This ain't right."

"There was nothing we could've done. He was already dead. No one could fix that."

"I am going to fix this. I'm calling the police."

"Don't you dare, Colton!" Regina screamed. "Colton!"

He stopped and turned. Regina was between him and the body, her breath heaving like an animal's.

"He was already dead. And...we need his blood."

"No..." Colton whispered.

"The harvest is near done. It won't grow again. You know it won't."

Colton shook his head. "Not like this, Regina."

"There's no other way, Colton. You promised me! You promised!"

Colton turned back towards the house. "No, Regina."

"Colton! Colton!"

He ignored her.

As he reached the house, he saw a flash of movement behind him, a reflection in the window.

THWACK.

Something hard struck the back of his head. All feeling disappeared as everything went white. His body collapsed to the ground.

CHAPTER 6

Colton's eyes fluttered open. He licked his parched lips, flies buzzing around his face. He felt a deep pressure in his head, like it was being pulled away from the rest of his body. All he could see were white and brown blurs, like he had opened his eyes underwater. His entire being was filled with ache. A soft squeak as he swayed in the light wind. He couldn't move.

His vision slowly focused. White sky. Dirt. The crop, a mixture of green and brown. Someone moving by the stalks. He was hanging upside down.

Colton groaned.

The figure by the stalks turned and walked towards him.

Regina clicked into focus, her sundress drifting with every step. She was covered in blood. In her right hand was a butcher knife. Her skin was so white it looked like a wet hole that had been rubbed into a painting.

"Colton..."

She walked over and steadied him, hanging upside down from a hook. His wrists were bound tight behind him, the burn of the rope digging into his skin. Directly below him was a large, metal tub.

Colton's cracked, dry lips barely cooperated with his will to speak. "What's happening, Regina?"

"Oh, Colton..." Tears of red began to flow from her eyes, staining the white of her skin. She wiped her face.

"What's happened to you, Regina?" he pleaded. Every inch of his body burned.

"I made a promise. These fields. This... This is who I am. This is...*what* I am."

"We'll make this work. Together."

"No..." She shook her head. "You couldn't do it. You

promised but you couldn't." She sobbed, her face stained red.

Colton contorted in pain. "I tried. I tried to do that. I tried. I tried…" Tears streamed down his face, dropping into the tub below with a soft, metallic patter.

Regina pressed her face against his, holding him close as their tears intertwined.

"I know you did, Colton. I know you did."

She raised the knife and ripped it across his neck.

She held him tight, her face pressed against his as blood streamed from the opening, enveloping them in a sheen of dark red.

Colton felt only warmth. His breathing stopped, pressure building in his lungs as they grasped for air. A soft gurgle from the wound.

Regina whispered as she cradled his body. "You'll be with me forever. You don't have to try anymore. You don't have to be something you're not."

She held him tight as Colton drained out, his blood pouring into the metallic tub below.

Regina took a step back, wiping the coat of red from her eyes. She turned and walked slowly back to the crop.

Colton watched her go, the sensation in his neck pulsing with heat. He slowly faded away as he swayed in the soft breeze, ears filled with the sound of his insides hitting the floor of the metal tub.

Regina walked into the crop, the hard earth painted red. She lowered herself to the ground. The leaves of the stalks bobbed in the wind. She spread open her hands and dug them into the soil, clutching the dirt between her fingers.

THE BURRYMAN

By Mackenzie Hurlbert

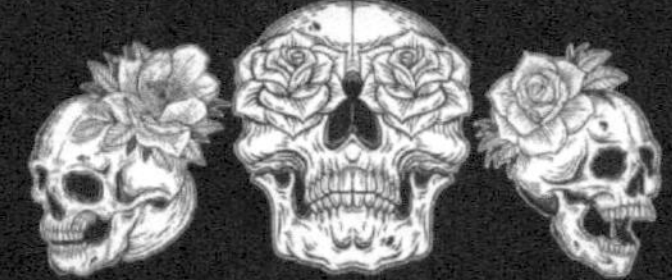

"A tipple for the Burryman," Widow Summers whispers, as she pours the honey wine between Colin's lips.

Despite her unsteadiness these days, her knob-knuckled hand stays precise. She's careful not to splash his balaclava. Once the burs around his face grow sweet and fragrant, the bees will come calling.

A small gap in the mask grants access to his mouth, and through the eyeholes, his gaze softens as he savors the drink. The rest of my brother, every patch of skin except for his hands, is covered in cloth and then a thick layer of burs. He is a mound of barbed greenery, the hard angles of him softened and rounded. His arms stretch out to either side, grasping two heavy staffs topped with flowers and vines. It is my job, and our cousin John's, to guide his steps. We walk on either side and share the staffs with him to ensure he stays standing, a difficult task following a day of drink and rambling.

Though, maybe this year won't be so much of a challenge. The Widow's the first one to greet us along the path—the first in almost an hour of walking. Colin's been the Burryman for nearly eight years in a row now—voted in each time like the local authorities, facing no opposition—and each spring, those who honor the tradition grow fewer and fewer. In years past, we'd be reaching the Widow's house closer to midday from all the stops and pictures and offerings. It's barely 9am, and we're almost through a third of the village.

When the Widow's done, she threads some flowers in among his suit of burs—purple violets that cling easily in the tines and yellow primrose. A bur catches on her sleeve as she pulls away. I pause to pluck it off and return it to Colin's side.

"Thank you, ma'am," I say, nodding, and guide Colin away from her gate and back to the main road.

When we're well on our way up the hill, John sighs. The next words he speaks are just a whoosh of breath. "I'm just about done, Cousins."

"What's that supposed to mean?" I ask, refusing to slow my pace.

I use my free hand to swipe my curls from my face and curse myself for forgetting a hair tie. Beside me, Colin stays silent; the Burryman should never speak. That was one of the many traditions the last Burryman passed down to him—no speaking, always drink what's offered, and do not stop until you've passed by every home in the village. Those in the village who honor the tradition, like Widow Summers, are expected to offer a drink for the Burryman. Wreaths and garlands are also accepted, though many just pluck wildflowers from the roadside.

"This," John says, waving a hand at me and Colin. "It was fun and all when we started, but no one cares anymore. And I'm nearly forty. I'm missing my son's football game right now; Monica's right pissed about it. And all for what? So old Widow Summers can pour a gravy boat of mead down Colin's throat?"

We near another house with a car in the driveway. Stopping at the front gate, I see two children watching from an upstairs window. I wave, smiling. They turn away and let the curtain fall.

"See?" John says. "Even the kids are over it. We're three

grown adults wandering around beggin' for a drink. Maybe a hundred years ago, people had nothing better to do. Hell, even fifty years ago, this was probably the most exciting day in town. But everyone's busy now. Even my kid's got an itinerary on the kitchen wall for his weekly commitments, and he's eight."

We wait for the kids to come downstairs, for the parents to open the door and rush out with apologies and a juice box or a warm beer. When nothing happens, we turn and continue up the hill through the center of the village.

I spy the red roof and brownstone of the Historical Center, and my heart softens. As a child, I found my passion within those walls. Now the only caretaker, I pride myself on nurturing the same wonder. This spring we have an exhibit of dried flowers and garlands dating back to the early 1900s—all once tokens for the Burryman. Paired with the black and white images I printed on large canvases and a pair of old spectacles worn by the Burryman of 1928, I believe it makes for quite a nice exhibit...

Not that many have stopped in to see it.

I shift my grasp on the staff and fight back a grimace. "Well, John," I say, not bothering to hide the bite from my voice. "We'll make sure to count you out for next year."

"Ahh, don't be so sour about it, Marsha." John reaches behind Colin and claps me on the shoulder. "Maybe you'll find a life by then. You know, a nice boy, a hobby. Something more worth your time than that dusty museum and this bullshit."

His laughter echoes in the empty street.

I grit my teeth and keep walking, my grip tightening on the staff. Since when did old world say, "Screw tradition?" Sure, I don't have much going on, and sure, I have no need for a weekly planner. But even if I did have a partner of my own or a family or whatever, I would still find time for Burryman Day, to continue what our fathers once did, and their fathers before them. To complete a yearly ritual so long engrained in our village's history that no one really knows why or how it started.

I think of those black and white prints blown up on the Historical Center's walls and the dark hollows of the Burryman's eyes.

"I will be here next year, don't you doubt that," I grumble, as we pass another house, its shutters drawn and yard empty.

We keep walking, looping through neighborhoods and stopping at a few more homes. First, an older couple offers Colin some beer through a straw, then a family greets us, and the child holds up a CapriSun pouch. We walk for another hour before the next villager meets us at his front step and pours a finger of whiskey down Colin's throat. The man's russet hound waits patiently by the door and thumps his tail in greeting.

"That's the good stuff," the old-timer mumbles, removing his straw hat and nodding to Colin before we move on.

The sun's high as we pass under the shade of an oak. Colin's breathing heavily beside me.

John sighs and slows. "Oddly warm for May, innit?" When neither Colin nor I respond, he grumbles something that sounds like, "Another reason to be done with this..."

Colin stops, facing John with his whole body as the burs make it impossible for him to turn his head.

"You're not the one covered in fuckin' burs, you know," he mutters.

John grunts a laugh. I turn as if Colin slapped me.

"What the hell, Colin?!"

"What?!" he says, pivoting to face me.

"Don't 'What?' me! You know the Burryman's not s'posed to speak."

"Eh! Give it up, Marsh."

John chuckles once more behind him, and I debate tackling him into the nearby rhododendron bush.

The mound of green before me—Colin—shrugs. He carefully peels off his bur-covered balaclava, the one I spent nearly an hour covering this morning behind the Historical Center. A few years ago, I cultivated a handful of small burdock plants there for convenience on Burryman Day, yes, but also because I love the reminder they provide on the other days of the year. My fingers are still sore from plucking the burs and nestling them in place.

One catches on the hairs of his hand and he winces, shaking the thing off with a flick. Red-faced and wide-eyed, Colin faces me and shrugs again. Sweat trickles down his forehead. His eyes are the color of mud. "I think I'm done too."

He lets go of each staff and walks back toward the village center, arms held away from his sides like a coasting gull. John passes me his staff and follows.

I am speechless. John had been doing this for nearly a decade, Colin and I a tad less. Our father had been a Burryman, and our grandfather too. And just like that, the tradition's over? They can't, I think. It's a tradition for a reason. It's been done for over a hundred years; it should continue on for a hundred more. I scramble after them, struggling with the two staffs.

"What, is the drink not good enough for you? Not high-shelf enough?" I shout, catching up as they shuffle back home. "You honestly have no respect for tradition? For ritual? For history, even?" In my arms, the staffs are awkward and heavy, shedding petals in my wake.

Colin turns. "No, Marsh, I honestly don't, and no one else seems to give a damn either. Why bother doing it if no one cares? I feel a fool wandering around in my thermals covered in burs and flowers." He plucks one of Widow Summer's violets from his chest and tosses it to the ground. "It's over. Someone else can be the Burryman next year."

Bastards, I think, and stop walking.

They disappear around a corner hedge. I chuck the staffs into the ditch along the road and sit on the curb, watching the row of quiet houses. Crashing through the silence, a group of teenagers drive by, all of them piled in a small Volkswagen and singing at the top of their lungs to the radio. A bee buzzes past, circling for a moment before moving on. The rest of the neighborhood is still. The sun is high, but no one's outside to enjoy its warmth. The flowers are in bloom, but there are no children here to pick them or offer them to the Burryman.

Does no one care? I wonder, rising to my feet.

Just me, I guess, and Widow Summers, and the villager in the straw hat. That couple with the Capri-Sun child. Very few of us, but at least we're here.

I dust the dirt from my jeans and walk back the way we came, stopping into the liquor store as I make my way through town. I buy a bottle of their finest port, its deep blood color nearly glowing in the sunlight. It costs me a day's pay but hell, what other occasions do I have to celebrate, right? I crack the bottle open, taking a deep pull as I cross through town.

I pass the cool shadows of the Historical Center, then meander through the outskirts of the village and up the hillside. The path's overgrown, less used than in years past, but I traipse through to reach my favorite clearing near the hilltop.

I pause, breathing deep. The grass here smells sweet, and the cool breeze brushes the hair from my face as I take a seat and overlook the village. I drink until my head buzzes with a thousand bees, and then I lie back, tucking the bottle in the crook of my arm, and close my eyes to apologize to my father and grandfather and all the Burrymen before them.

I send out an apology to whoever started the ritual—maybe the pagans whose marks left deep grooves in the cliffs nearby—and explain that I tried. I really did. I let the sun warm my already ruddy face, inhale deeply, and fall asleep with those apologies on my lips.

I awake sometime later to a goat keening.

Is it a goat?

My eyes flutter open as I register the chill, and the dark clouds rolling over the village below. I stand, letting my head catch up to my body, and the bottle topples and rolls loose. The last glugs of wine seep into the grass and dirt. Another wail cuts through the air, no doubt human as I shake my mind clear.

Above, the day's blue sky has transformed into a slate of storm clouds. The air grows thick and tingly, as if the breeze itself has turned into a static current.

I set off in a run to the village below.

When I see the first row of houses at the end of the trail, my breath hitches. The yards of the homes around me have withered and yellowed. The lush patchwork of grass the residents so carefully fertilize and manicure has shriveled into wisps of dead blades and balding spots of dusty earth. The rhododendron bushes are skeletal arms and scraggly fingers of branches. Their evergreen leaves skitter across the pavement.

The wailing sounds once more from one street over and I run, trying to make sense of the window boxes of withered flowers and the sudden bite in the air. The storm clouds rumble as I duck through a gate and follow the sound of sobbing to the backyard. A young girl and her mother kneel in the dirt while the father holds a cellphone to his ear.

"I was—" I start to say.

The mother turns, her hand circling her daughter's back. "What do you want?"

Her eyes are hard as if I'm some door-to-door salesman peddling solar panels or window replacements.

"I just heard…" I step closer, spying a white mound in the grass by their knees. "Is everything okay?"

"Oh," she says, her eyes darting to the grass. "It was my daughter. We, uh… We lost our rabbit just now."

I take another step closer, and the child looks up at me, tears dribbling down her cheeks. Her ice-blue eyes shine bright and unnatural, her face red and furrowed with sorrow. She raises two tiny, clenched fists toward me, then shakes them to her rabbit. The animal is still, flopped on one side as if asleep.

"He just fell over," the child wails, between gasps for breath. "He just fell over and died."

With that, she breaks into a deeper round of sobs, and the mother turns to comfort her. I step back once, and then again, my sneakers crunching on the dead grass.

The father walks past, muttering into the phone, "I don't know what caused it, Tom. We just came out here, the yard's gone to shit, and she's screaming her head off." He pauses. "You too, huh? Yellow and dusty? I've never seen anything like it."

Above, the clouds rumble once more.

I take off running toward Village Center. Colin has probably gravitated to the pub by now, and maybe he's heard what caused all this. Each yard I pass on my way there is dead and yellow. In one, a coop full of chickens sits still and silent, their feathered bodies sprawled in the dust. I swallow back a wave of nausea and push on, running through the neighborhood until I spy one yard that's unlike the rest.

One home's left unbothered, its grass still green, and the small trellis of morning glory by the door as vibrant and blooming as when I stopped by earlier. The russet hound who thumped his tail in greeting continues to watch the road and offers a friendly bay as I stop in the street. The man in the straw hat is reading on his front step and looks up to meet my stare.

No smile, no wave.

When I do nothing, he refocuses on the book in his lap. A heavy breeze pushes dried leaves across the pavement as I turn and pick up my pace.

I'm crossing the street toward the pub when I hear John calling my name. He's jogging to meet me. The air feels thick and electrified, and while the clouds shroud much of the sun, the world around us has this odd, sepia glow. I blink a few times trying to chase it away, but it's no trick of my vision.

"Where the hell've you been?" John shouts, his voice higher pitched in panic. He's got me by the elbow now, and I feel his clammy palms through the thin fabric of my shirt.

I look around. The streets are full of my neighbors and fellow villagers, some staring wide-eyed at the dying world around them, others rushing off to their homes. "Where is my brother?"

"Reporting for duty," Colin says, emerging from the pub. He's shed the suit of burs for a t-shirt and a pair of cargo shorts. From the sway in his walk, I can tell he'd been indulging since we'd split earlier. "What'd I miss?"

I look from him to John. "What the hell happened?"

Colin burps and scratches his neck. "I just came out to see what all the shouting's been 'bout."

John's got us both by an elbow and starts pulling us down the sidewalk. "It was like a wave. One minute, I'm on the phone with Monica, looking out the window, and the next, the yard's turning yellow like a toxic spill. I actually saw it seep across the lawn. The trees all dropped their leaves. A flock of birds flew into the picture window out front and broke their necks. Not one, but a whole flock of them. I couldn't believe it."

He stops and wipes a bead of sweat from his lip. I read the panic in his eyes, and my heart thunders in response.

"It was like that everywhere," I say quietly. "All except that last house we stopped at. The one with the hound. Have either of you passed Widow Summers' house? Or that family that greeted us?"

They shake their heads no.

Colin watches me, eyes wide. "What're you saying?"

John is silent.

"It's tradition for a reason, you know."

I whisper the words, but they both hear me.

Colin shakes his head and steps back, forcing out a laugh. "Oh please, Marsh."

I open my mouth to protest, but Colin's laughter turns into a thick, wet cough. His shoulders start to quake and soon his whole body convulses with each hack. My hand is on his shoulder, and I feel the shudder of each cough course through my palm. His rosy cheeks grow a deep red, and his eyes pinch in pain. He coughs and coughs and coughs, and when he manages to breathe, the inhale wheezes through his chest.

John's trying to get us moving again. Back toward his

house, he says. He's pulling my arm and shoving Colin, but after a few steps, Colin bends over again and continues hacking.

This time, spit flies from the corners of his mouth. I hear a thick gurgle from somewhere deep within him as he crouches low, like a child inspecting an ant on a blade of grass. He takes one more wheezing breath and then heaves between his knees. A mound of burs and mucus splatter across the sidewalk at his feet.

He looks up at me, tears in his eyes and lips bloody. He nods.

"Burryman," he croaks, before bowing his head once more and vomiting a heavy stream of burs and bile onto the ground.

He moans, falling to all fours. I take a step back as lightning flashes overhead and the sky rumbles. The wind whips my hair across my face and I tear at it, fighting to tuck it behind my ears.

I look up to find John's running away now. He's sprinting down the road and scrambling around other groups trying to get home, parked cars, and people on bicycles. Lightning cracks again.

All at once, the world around me is filled with drumbeats, the percussion of fist-sized hailstones hitting pavement, garbage cans, and people. I hover over Colin, shielding him as best I can, and watch John run until a stone the size of a softball falls from the sky above and clocks him in the head. He drops, stunned, but then I see him start to crawl. I hear a woman yelp in the distance. Hail bounces off my lower back and I gasp at the pain.

"Colin," I grind out, "we need to move."

He's a shivering mess below me. He heaves once more, and a clump of burs falls from his lips. Droplets of red bile sprinkle my sneakers.

Another hailstone slams into my shoulder. I grab him by the collar and drag him a few steps up the sidewalk until we're under the tin awning of a storefront. The thunder of hail hitting the metal roof is deafening. I shout at Colin to stay where he is, and then I turn to survey the street around me.

It's empty. Everyone's scattered for their homes, or they've holed up in the pub or laundromat. Through the foggy windows of the coffee shop, I see pale faces peering out at me. The hail continues, pummeling down on the village, dealing blow after blow to whatever it finds.

Nearby, I watch a sizeable stone crash into a car windshield. The glass splinters into a spiderweb of cracks. At my feet, Colin continues to heave. The stream of burs grows bloodier.

"It's tradition for a reason," I murmur to myself, and shoot out from under the awning as fast as my legs can carry me.

I run close to the buildings and follow the sidewalk around the corner until I'm at the Historical Center, its dark windows overlooking the street like two sleepy eyes. A hailstone crashes into the back of my head and I stagger, seeing purple for a moment. I duck into the alley beside the Center and only stop when I reach the patch of bur plants.

They claim the entire garden plot, and while the yards, trees and shrubs around us are yellowed and brittle, the overgrowth of burdock waits, green and golden in the distorted light of the storm. Another hailstone collides with my shoulder, but I ignore the pain that follows.

Instead, I dive headfirst into the patch.

Branches claw my skin. A sharp point drags across my forehead. Others pierce my clothes and dig into my legs and arms. I fall further and know I've found the burs when it feels like a thousand tiny jaws are biting and tugging on me. They latch onto the soft weave of my shirt and nestle in my curls. They scratch across my neck as I wriggle deeper into the thicket.

I hiss as the fragile skin on the back of my hands grows red and raw. My ankles. My cheeks. All the soft exposed parts of me burn as I rise to my feet. My hair catches painfully in the bushes below, but I tug free, fighting back tears.

The dried point of a branch dislodges from my thigh, and I wince as a warm bloom of blood spreads through the fabric of my jeans.

Stepping free from the patch, I check to make sure I'm covered. There are a handful of clumps on my legs, and a few burs cling to the laces and mesh of my shoes, but at least my shirt has been well coated. My hair no longer sways freely behind me; it lies matted and heavy on my neck and against my cheeks. Blood trickles down the side of my face. I can feel it gather and drip from my chin but don't bother wiping it away.

Let them see what this costs.

I leave the clearing behind the Historical Center and walk back toward where I left Colin, my steps careful and deliberate. With each movement, I feel the tines of the burs digging through my shirt. I fight the urge to itch, to wriggle in discomfort. I just walk while the hail slows. The village folk waiting in the storefronts around me watch my approach and emerge, wide-eyed and trembling.

As the clouds start to clear, the first one to approach me is a young woman with her work apron still tied around her waist. Her hair's pulled back in a tight bun, and a smear of blood stains her temple. She lifts a bottle of Coke to my lips and pours. I savor the mouthful, letting the carbonation tickle the inside of my cheeks before swallowing. She nods her head and rushes away, and I say nothing as the next villager steps up. This one slips a flask from his back pocket and pours the strong, bitter liquor between my lips until I hold up a hand for him to stop.

Soon, the street is full of villagers lined up on either side, waiting their turn to share their offerings. I move from one to the next and focus on the cool liquid I swallow and the burn that often follows.

With each step, the burrs chafe and dig into me, clawing the hollows of my neck as I tilt my head to drink. My wounded thigh throbs, a slow, persistent ache. I roll my shoulders back and push away the pain.

Catching a glimpse of my reflection in a shop window, I pause.

My red-streaked face peers out from a mane of burrs. Around me, broken glass glitters on the pavement like parade confetti. Someone clears their throat and I turn to find Colin waiting, a bottle in his hand. His lips are scratched raw, but his face has regained a bit of color. I smile as he pours a mouthful of port, waits for me to swallow, and then offers another.

"Had to go fetch it from the pub," he says, his voice hoarse. He shares a lopsided grin, though his eyes still hold a spark of fear as he adds, "I'm not sure what the Burryman prefers, but I do know it's your favorite."

He offers an arm to hold and keeps pace as I walk onward.

John shares apologies with his tipple, peering out from beneath his bandage, before he squeezes my hand and bows his head. I release him and move along, drinking and shifting from one villager to the next.

I don't recognize them all, but I do recognize their fear and awe. Their respect.

At one stop, a girl with a bloodied nose places a circlet of woven willow branches on my head. At the next, an older man offers his walking stick as a staff. With each step, I notice buds sprout from the bare limbs of the trees and shrubs, bright with the promise of new life.

I pause for another offering, kneeling so the child can hold the drink to my lips. I swallow hard and Colin helps me rise. We need to keep moving if I'm going to reach the rest of the village before nightfall.

For now, though, there's a cloudless sky above, and the sun waits high over the hilltop, gilding the world in its light. I breathe deeply and crunch a skittering leaf beneath my next step.

THE NIGHTMARE EXCHANGE

By Sarah Day

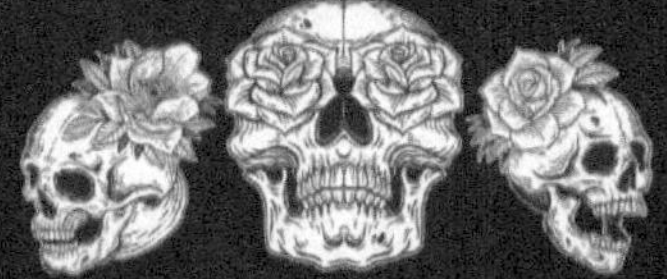

The geist had haunted Magda's family for three generations. It had taken root in her grandpa after he near-drowned when a skiff overturned. The geist rode him up from the bottom of the bog, erupting into daylight when he broke the swamp's algae-dotted surface, wreathed in weeds and coughing up black bile. It was inside him all his life...

Until his daughter bled for the first time, and the geist seeped out of him and into her.

The geist drowned Magda's childhood. Both her mother and grandfather were old before their years from sleeplessness and creaky-voiced from screaming. Neither swam. Neither could go on a boat. Her mother wouldn't even go outside when it rained.

When Magda came of age, the geist came to live in her. It swam through her sleep, giving her screaming nightmares of weeds binding her to the swamp floor, silt swallowing her limbs, dark water in her throat. She tried to trick it, avoiding sleep with teas and night fishing and distraction, but it always prevailed. Potions to quell her dreaming didn't work either; the geist was strong and fat on her family's terror. It found her everywhere.

Magda saw her family's life laid out before her and did not want it.

Hag Wendy, the bog witch, took Magda's three remaining baby teeth as payment. When that proved insufficient, she demanded two ounces of menstrual blood and danced with glee to have the end of childhood and the beginning of adulthood from the same person.

The enchantments to pull the geist out of Magda had taken three moon cycles, one for each generation the geist had ridden, but the result was her family's nightmare, now bound and fettered in a thick, glass jar. It was dark grey-green, barely translucent, with one stripe of bright eggshell blue wrapped around its circumference. When she held it, it hummed against her skin.

She showed the jar to the spearman guarding the gates of the New Moon Carnival as proof she had something to sell. Her people had little magic and less coin, and did not go to Carnivals as a rule, but Hag Wendy had said a friend of hers who worked the Carnival might be intrigued by a geist.

The arched gate was painted in red and gold and violet, faded and worn, but still brighter colors than ever she saw in the swamp. She did her best to ignore the man's expression of disdain as he stepped aside and let her in.

The Carnival was a ramble of colorful awnings and long tables of wares, broken here and there by vendors with rugs spread on the ground. Magda paused in the aisle and considered her choices. On one side, an enchanted toad salesman—"Need a curse broken? Eat a toad and hop to it!"—and on the other, a troupe of memory harvesters, their faces shrouded, an array of silver picks and scalpels laid out and shiny on a table. They were doing fast and bloody business with a line of grim-faced customers outside their booth, each of them presumably holding a memory in their heads they needed to be rid of.

"Here, now. That's a familiar jar."

The voice was pitched to land in Magda's ears. She turned

to see an elderly woman perched on a stool behind a nearby table.

"Come over here, child. You have the look of the bog about you."

Magda saw something familiar in the old woman too. The tattered spiderweb lace and gator teeth bracelets, the skirts and blouses layered to disguise that each individual piece was mostly holes, the tortoiseshell combs holding back a river of curly silver hair.

"Are you Hag Wendy's friend?" She groped for the name. "Salla?"

The woman chortled. "I'm she, although 'round these parts they call me the Swamp Witch. You have one of Wendy's geist jars, girl. Them don't come cheap."

Magda fingered the jar, bulging though the net bag that hung off her shoulder. "I do, and they don't. I'm looking to swap it."

"Is it multigenerational?" She snorted at Magda's blank look. "A family geist, child. Did it sit with your mama and her mama and her mama until it came down to you? Here—"

With a deft twist of her crabbed fingers, Salla reached out and plucked the cork from the geist jar's neck.

Magda yelped, dropped to her knees, and fumbled the jar out of the string bag. It jumped out of her nerveless fingers and thudded on the sod, the geist bleeding out with a sigh that sounded relieved. It flowed across the grass and up Magda's skirts, the cool sensation pouring wrong-ways up her body. She couldn't *not* look at it bleeding up her clothes. It was the color of the sky between stars, of the bottom of the bog. As it approached her face, she heard the roar of the sea's depths. Its webbed touch felt like wet kelp and heavy water.

She bit back her terror and plunged her hands into the geist, scooping up its cold, ethereal limbs as best she could and funneling it back into the jar with her fingers. Where was the cork? Where? One scrambling hand found it on the ground between her and Salla, and shoved it back into the neck of the bottle hard, mashing an errant loop trying to climb out.

She bent her body over the jar as the geist rioted inside, furious. The jar shivered and quaked. It raged like a hurricane.

The geist wanted nothing more than to climb back aboard her body, the sweetest and most familiar ride it knew. Horrified by how close it had come, Magda pressed both palms down over the cork and glared at Salla through furious tears.

"How dare—"

Salla kicked her heels out on her stool, cackling. "Look at that sharp fellow, all teeth and bad intention. Whoo! Lots of market for the little hauntlings what attach to you after a bad night's sleep or on a long trip out in the bayou, but *that* nasty treat? Family geists are harder to shift. They get strong on all that ready food."

Magda swallowed the rock in her throat. Her heart slammed like a doomed fish against the bottom of a boat. "But do you want it?"

Salla chuckled and sucked on her pipe. "Chuck it into the bog, for all it's worth to me."

"I can't!" She heard the desperation in her voice and hated it. "The geist will just follow me home unless I can entice it to look at someone else. You don't know anyone who would want it?"

Salla rolled her pipe stem from one gap in her smile to another. "Child, most folk here don't want what they already have."

The rest of the morning was wasted.

She tried the rare animal dealers, with their tanks of bright fish and cages of baby bog leopards. They even had a white gator. They would only take living things, the man stressed, leaning as far away from the jar as he could without falling off his stool.

The anesthetists, with their thick gloves, were busy smearing numbing unguent on troublesome limbs and eyes and hearts. They ignored her.

There were sweet dream vendors, each promising peaceful nights and joyful mornings with more vehemence than the last. None wanted the geist.

Magda's feet and eyes ached. Inside the bag, the geist rattled and danced.

The distillers were in a long yard fenced off by rope lines abutting the waterline. Three people, two men and a woman, hovered around the enormous copper tank, which was longer than they were tall and nearly their height. Tasks whose purpose she couldn't identify occupied them—adjusting valves, pouring a viscous clear liquid into a hole in the top, arranging a dingy bunting on their table in front of the still. The table boasted a sign, red and white, with words Magda couldn't read.

"Shoo off, girl-miss," the man at the table said. "We ain't cooking yet. Boiler is heating. It'll be an hour."

Magda continued her approach, drawing the geist jar out of the bag. "I ain't here to buy. I have this to sell or swap, if you're interested."

The man stopped his preparations and gave her, and the jar, his full attention.

He was greasy-faced and stubbly, his eyes and teeth all sharp and yellow. He looked badly underslept, but his clothes were bright, rich mossy green and russet red, and even if there were stains on his shirt, it was a fine linen shirt, with glass buttons besides. Her own brown drab and wooden buttons felt clumsy and childlike.

"What's this now?" he asked, bending down to inspect the jar closely, as if he had bad eyesight. Magda smelled soap, sharp and spicy, and underneath that, body odor.

"Is this a memory jar, girl?" He grinned up at her lasciviously. "Are you selling something sweet? Your first time dancing at a country fair? Losing your virginity in the bottom of your father's rowboat? Pretty girl like you, I bet you have all sorts of fine memories."

Magda flushed hot. "It's a geist jar, sir. It's my family nightmare what I want to be rid of."

The man bounced back, hands up, an exaggerated display of intimidation. "A geist jar! My goodness gracious. What terrible nightmares must they have in these swamps? A croaking frog keeps you up all night? A rushlight you chase and fades out with sunrise? Moss that grows between your toes, no matter how you scrub?"

Infuriated, Magda thrust the jar up in front of his face, thumb tight over the cork, and shook it. The geist woke and growled at the mistreatment, darkening the clouded glass to black. The rush of water filled her ears. Lightning flickered inside the jar, which buzzed and rattled in her hand as if it were full of hornets.

The man stared, transfixed, and when she pulled the jar out of view, he twitched. From this distance, she could tell he was sweating.

"It's a geist of drowning," she said, probably unnecessarily. "And it's been sitting with my family twoscore years. It ain't no loose-tooth dream."

The man stared at her as if not understanding her, then composed himself. "You're not wrong. You have the genuine article there, don't you?"

"I do. And I wish to be rid of it."

He leaned back on hearing that, looked down his stubby nose at her, appraising. "And what do you think I might be able to do with it?"

Her eyes flickered to the ruddy still, the assistants working at the boilers and valves. "I don't know. Maybe you could distill it, turn it into something you could use."

A predatory eagerness lit in his eyes. She had asked him for something, and in so doing, bared her throat to him. "A geist so strong is dangerous. I maybe could use it, refine it into something, run it through the still a few times. Still, that's much work for me, effort and danger for uncertain reward. So, I ask—" At this, he reached out, clucked her gently under the chin, tilted her face up toward the watery, grey sky. "What else can you do for me?"

She shied away. "Forget it. Nothing. I'll find someone else."

He barked a laugh. "Not here you won't, little girl. No one will take a geist like that from you. To be ridden by that, you might as well drown yourself, for someday it surely will."

He leaned back from her, tucked his thumbs into his belt, gave her an appraising up-and-down.

"I'm Creach. I can take anything, plant or liquid or dream or nightmare or ghost, and turn it into a dram. How's this? I take the geist; you work the stills with me for a season. Be rid of your nightmare, and learn a trade besides. Three fulls and empties of the moon, that's all." He smiled enticingly. "What's that, to rid yourself of a lifetime of nightmares?"

Cradling the geist jar against her chest, Magda considered it. Three fulls and empties of the moon was what it had taken to wrest the geist out of her body and into this jar. While it had been a long season, being able to sleep the night away was a gift beyond price. What was another three months to be rid of it for good?

She weighed the jar in her hands, felt the heft of it. The glass was cool and heavy, no longer shaking. Perhaps the geist was thinking too.

Creach backed into the yard, beckoning, and she drifted warily behind him. He was looking at her like she was a chicken dinner. The two workers, loose-skinned and yellow-eyed like Creach, were busily preparing the still. As she watched, one fumbled a dipper bucket and dropped it, splashing liquid all over the ground.

"Watch yourself, Liza!" Creach barked, in a much different voice than he'd been speaking to Magda. The puddle of liquid on the ground hissed faintly and shivered with bubbles.

The woman bent to right the bucket in a series of slow, clumsy motions. She moved like she was much older than she looked, paused halfway down to rock a bit back and forth, like she had lost her sense of balance.

Magda peered through the puddle of golden liquid and watched blades of grass shrivel and wilt.

"We make all sorts of concoctions. Three different chambers, so we can cook different recipes at once, or open it up to make one thing in a batch. Depends on what we're contracted to do. Here—"

Creach pried the top off a wooden crate. Inside, an array of fluted glass bottles sat under a thin layer of straw.

The bottle he removed was a soft rose color, the prettiest glass Magda had ever seen. Creach took a metal circle from a pocket in his vest. It telescoped out into a tiny tin cup. He uncorked the bottle with a flourish and poured the liquid into the cup with great care.

Creach tipped a measure into his mouth and offered the cup to Magda. "Try some yourself."

Magda looked into the cup. The dram, deep gem red, smelled delicious, like berries and bog flowers in spring. She knew better than to take a glass from a man she didn't know, but he'd drunk from it already, so what could be the harm? She raised it to her lips and sipped.

Sensation burst on her tongue and coursed through her body, from mouth to throat to fingertips and toes. Motes of golden light crept in from the edge of her vision like fireflies wakening at dusk. Creach's face was illuminated from within by a soft glow. He wasn't as rundown looking as she'd first thought. His skin was smooth and youthful, his eyes bright green like foxfire. Nearly handsome.

It was very forward to stare at a man like this, but he was smiling, so he must not mind. Magda heard herself giggle. She tipped the cup to her lips again, caught a last drop from the bottom. It was delicious, as happy and easy as being a child again, like the times she had maybe made up, maybe remembered, before the geist. Before anything bad had happened.

Inside the bag, the geist buzzed, faint and even as a purr. She touched the jar with awe, her fingers newly sensitive to the glass's smooth surface.

"My geist could make something like this?"

"This is one of many things the still can do," Creach said. "Your geist wouldn't be suited for this, exactly. But something like it, something what suggests feelings in whoever drinks it."

Magda squinted at him. The firefly lights were fading, disappearing in tiny pops like soap bubbles. "What kind of feelings?"

Creach shifted his weight from one foot to another. "Could be many things. Every batch's a little different."

The woman at the still was sneering at her, and the open disdain cut through the dreamy easiness in Magda's mind. She shook herself, the last of the dram's effects dissipating. She scrubbed her eyes with one hand and the last of the firefly lights vanished. Creach was staring at her with hunger.

"Try another."

As much as she wanted to be rid of the geist, something in her bowels said, *not this man*. Whatever he claimed to give her, she thought, he wanted to take more.

Magda took two big steps backwards, out from behind the table, away from the still. "Thank you for talkin' to me. I'll think about it."

Creach startled. He caught her elbow as she turned away and pulled her back. "Hey now, girl-miss. I gave you a taste. You owe me the same."

This close, she could smell the still's by-products on his

breath, sour grapes and honey. The dram's effects were gone. His teeth were reedy green and his skin oily.

Magda pulled away. "Let me loose. You gifted me that little drop, I don't owe you nothing." She tried not to look afraid. He was much bigger than she and she didn't know what she would do if he pressed her.

Creach squeezed her elbow tighter. "No one here will take a nightmare like that but me. It would be a favor to you!"

Fear fluttered in her heart while the geist buzzed in counterpoint. She didn't know if Creach wanted the geist or her, or both, but she wanted nothing to do with him. She pulled back hard and spun on her heel, striding away from him as fast as she could without running.

The crowd closed around her. She sped up, one hand securing the jar in its bag as she took a sharp turn down a different aisle. She collided hard with someone else, a rude meeting of shoulders and elbows and chins. Something hit her hard in the stomach and she fell.

Magda landed on her ass, the wind knocked out of her. She swore, gasping and grabbing desperately at the geist jar to make sure it hadn't broken. It was whole, the cork still on. Inside, the geist hissed unhappily, staining the glass an oily grey-green.

Her assailant was a boy about her age, black-haired and stocky. "I'm so sorry! Wasn't looking where I was going. Just an accident."

Magda ignored him. She was too winded to get up yet, and there were busy feet all around her, so she crawled between two tables and concentrated on breathing. The boy stayed on the ground in the aisle, patting at his pockets.

As she watched, he produced a series of objects from—a fold of yellow paper money from a town she didn't know, a stub of candle and book of matches, a tiny, green jar banded in ominous blue. He ran his hands all over the outside of this last, fingers playing over it anxiously, feeling for chips or cracks.

Magda stared. The stripes of blue around his jar were

different from hers—many of them, and thin, rather than one thick one, and running top to bottom rather than 'round the middle—but the blue color was identical. The ethereal, ghostly blue of an old eggshell.

Geist blue.

"Is that...?"

He looked up at her, was nearly trampled by a drunk couple who weren't paying attention, and scrambled over to kneel next to her under the table.

"Are you hurt? I'm real sorry, I didn't even see you."

Magda reached into her bag with a shaking hand and pulled out the geist jar. Held next to his, the stripes were the same color, or near enough as to make no difference.

The boy stared, slack-jawed, at her.

"Where did you get one of those?"

"Paid for it, and dear enough." Now that she was breathing again, her body was beginning to hurt. She rubbed her elbow. "You could watch where you're going."

"I know, I'm sorry. I've never been to the Carnival before, and everything was so interesting... I'm Peter. Hello."

"Magda." She offered a grimy hand and they shook. "Is that your family geist?"

"My family? Dunno if it's my whole family, but it's my dad's for sure."

He hefted the little jar. Inside, a cloud of geist ripped and swirled through itself, a gleam of red piercing out of its core like a faraway star.

"He sent you with it to sell?"

"Sent it... Not really. Is this your first time at the Carnival?"

He smiled so guilelessly she almost didn't notice him changing the subject.

"Aye." She wriggled out from under the table, peeking about for signs of Creach. When none appeared, she lifted herself to her feet. "Been here all morning."

Peter stood up next to her. "Are we both trying to unload our geists?"

"And having a hell of a time of it."

"It's remarkable just to be here though, isn't it? I've heard about the Carnival since I was a boy, and it's everything I imagined it could be. It's nearly worth the trip by itself, to see all this." He gestured at a table full of pickled squab parts with undisguised glee.

Magda did not see anything wonderful about a table full of dead birds. She wanted to ask more questions, like how a boy with clean clothes and a city accent had a geist jar that was surely as born in the bog as hers was, but something made her bite her tongue. There was an egg in her mind with an idea inside, and cracks were appearing on its surface.

"What's been your favorite thing so far?"

Tangled in her thoughts, it took a minute for Magda to realize he was talking to her. She blinked. His exuberant cheer was jarring. "I... I dunno."

"Are you hungry? I saw some fried fish back a ways and I'd be happy to split some with you. No strings! An apology for knocking you down just now. Maybe you can tell me about your geist?"

She had just taken a 'no strings' sample from a man that ended up having strings anyway, and she was inclined to say no. But Peter's enthusiasm seemed so innocent she found herself consenting.

The fish were tiny, no longer than Magda's thumb, and fried in a batter that made them crispy. Peter bought a handful in a twist of waxed paper and they ate together, crunching through the flimsy bones and licking grease off their fingers. Magda was suddenly starving. When the fish were gone, she wished for more.

The idea continued hatching in her mind as Peter kept up a running commentary about everything he saw, with no awareness of volume or appearances. He was so transparently a newcomer. Magda wondered if this would even have occurred to her with someone more seasoned.

"...wish I'd had an easier time moving this jar, is all," he was saying, when she caught the monologue's thread again. "I could take it home and try to hide it, I guess, but I worry about it getting loose, and Dad... He shouldn't be around it. Bad for everyone."

"I know someone who would take it," Magda said, the words popping out of her mouth like someone else had spoken them. Just like that, the idea was out and shaking the wet off its wings.

Peter started, delight spreading across his cheeks. "You do? Magda! That's wonderful! Maybe I ran into you for a reason!"

She couldn't look directly at his face.

"Can you show me where they are? Introduce me, maybe?"

"Aye. Come on. It's this way."

She pushed past him, trying not to think further than the next few steps. Ridding herself of the geist, that was the thing. The most important thing.

The still was easy to see from far off, a shiny landmark set back from the dusty aisles. Peter followed Magda to it like a duckling.

Creach had looked at her with decidedly amorous interest. Magda looked back at Peter. He was a boy. It wouldn't be as bad for him.

Peter smiled cheerfully at her. She looked away, back toward the distillers' yard. She could do this. She'd already traded bone and blood and teeth to rid herself of the geist. She could trade him too.

"Over there."

She pointed, and he practically beat her to the yard.

Creach was atop the still, painstakingly turning a large valve with a wrench. When he saw Magda, he stopped his work and gave her a smug grin.

"Came to your senses, did ya?" he called across the yard.

"There's nowhere else but me, girl-miss. Ready to sign on full-time?"

"I have something even better for you." Magda elbowed Peter, who obviously had questions, but held up his jar. "A two-for-one deal."

"Two?" Creach left the wrench on the valve and slid down the ladder set against the still. "What you mean, two?"

"This is Peter. He has a geist too, and he's willing to work for you."

"What?" Peter said.

"Is he now? Come here, boy. Let me see that jar." Creach barely looked at Peter, but plucked the geist jar out of his hands. He shook the jar and squinted at the ruddy, red cloud inside. "Ain't as fearsome as yours, girl-miss. Dunno why I should take the trouble."

"That's the deal," Magda said. "You get mine too. Finder's fee. Take the two geists and Peter to work the still and we're square."

"What?" Peter looked back and forth between her and Creach. "What are you talking about?"

Magda was clenching her teeth so hard her jaw ached. She resolutely did not look at him. "Give him a taste of your wares, Creach. Like you did me."

Creach had ignored Peter up to this point, but now he stopped and gave Peter a solid look up and down. Something lit in his eyes, the same thing that had lit when he'd seen Magda.

"Aye, he's a strong lad, isn't he? Fine features too. Nice to look at across the yard. Hey, Liza! Winston! What do you think? Do we like the look of he?"

His call pulled the other two from the still. They gathered around Peter, one part curious and one part hungry. Liza plucked at his fine-spun shirt, felt the arm underneath. Creach shuffled off toward the wooden crates beside the still.

"Magda? What are they doing?" Peter flashed a frantic look over to her.

"I—" Magda didn't know what to say. "They'll take your geist, Peter. This is part of the bargain."

"But work for them? Go with them? I don't—hey!" Liza ran her hand down the back of Peter's thigh.

"Don't fret, boy." Creach was back with a mug much larger than the cup he'd shared with Magda. "Try a swallow of this and quiet down all those questions."

Peter's gaze flickered between Creach and Magda. He wiggled out from between Winston and Liza and hurried over next to her. Creach followed, pushing the mug into his hands.

"Don't worry about them," Creach said. "Be easy. They're harmless."

"Magda, what is this?"

Magda didn't know what to say. With the mug in one hand and the geist jar in the other, he looked like a little boy with toys too big for him. Magda's geist rattled against her hip. The time was now, if it was ever.

"Calm down," she said, through clenched teeth. "Have a drink."

Peter stared at her over the mug's rim as he swallowed, eyes full of questions. A familiar looseness came over his features.

"Wow," he said, and drank again. The workers watched him with undisguised jealousy.

"That's...really good."

Watching him, Magda felt sick. The ghost of the dram Creach had fed her curdled in her stomach.

"That's the spirit." Creach plucked the geist jar from his hand with the delicacy of a fox lifting an egg from the nest. "Not so fearsome, are we?"

Peter started to respond and got distracted. A dreamy smile curtained his face. "Are you gonna take my geist?"

"Yes we are, boy. And you're going to help us make it into something fresh and new. Does that sound nice?"

"Yeah. Nice."

"Come with me then." Creach put a fatherly hand on

Peter's shoulder and steered him into the yard.

"Hey, wait now!" Magda trotted after him. "You gotta take my geist!"

"And take it we shall, girl-miss. Once we've figured out the best way to distill it using Peter's little geist here." Creach threw her a cloying look over his shoulder. "Stick around, darlin'. We'll see what we can make of you."

Peter tossed a distracted look over his shoulder as he walked deeper into the yard, as if he'd been about to ask her something and couldn't remember what. Creach made a beeline for the still, pushed Peter gently toward the other two workers. Liza and Winston each caught one of Peter's arms in their clumsy hands. They walked away in lockstep. As Magda watched, Liza's free hand dropped to cup his ass. This time, Peter giggled.

"What will they do to him?"

"Once he sobers up? Teach him how to work the still. That and make burn salve. First couple weeks of distilling is about not dying from your own stupidity much as anything else. In the meantime...what they like. Don't worry. He'll enjoy it."

Magda was trembling. *He'll enjoy it.* She'd surely thought the same herself not an hour ago, but imagining it paled next to the real thing.

"Y'all are not one step better than slavers—"

Creach wheeled around, pointed his finger in Magda's face so hard and fast she nearly ran into it. "Don't you take that 'better'n you' tone with me, girl-miss. You knew what bargain you were striking when you brought him here. We'll do as we please. You sold him to us, sure as any slaver your own self."

Furious tears stung Magda's eyes. She had no footing here and she knew it. Creach flapped a dismissive hand at her in a 'wait here' gesture and followed the other three.

Peter vanished behind the still and Magda stood alone in the yard. She imagined herself with a mug of that liquor in her, the heat of the still on her breasts and belly, Creach's oily weight crushing her against it. This could have been her. *Would* have been, if she hadn't found Peter, if she hadn't brought Peter to them.

And she wouldn't have minded, the way Peter wasn't minding whatever was happening behind the still now.

Inside the jar, her geist buzzed. She touched the cork jammed into its neck and thought about her and her mother's and her grandfather's terror. She had brokered Peter into her nightmare exchange, and now that it was done, she knew she could not do it. Not and live with herself. Nightmares be damned.

Her geist was the black thing at the heart of the bottom of the bog, but the bog's depths couldn't be darker than this.

She was running before she had time to second-guess, one hand as always on the geist jar, steadying it against her hip. She rounded the end of the still with her mouth open, ready to offer a plea or argument or further negotiation, only to see Peter on his back on the ground, Liza and Winston crouched over him like vultures.

Magda hit them both square with her shoulders and all three went over together. As Peter started to sit up, a flailing knee or elbow hit his nose with a crack. He went back over with Magda on top of him.

Someone grabbed the back of her dress and yanked her up. Creach shook her so hard that her teeth cracked together, swearing at her. In the wake of his boozy, sour breath, her head swam. Her geist jumped like a bullfrog in the jar. Creach pulled a thick fist back to hit her, but before he did, Peter—up and clumsy, with a bloody nose, but moving fast—staggered into him and knocked both Creach and Magda down.

Her head hit the ground. She heard something shatter and thought it must be her skull. She opened her eyes to ruddy smoke seeping out from under Creach's prone body and thought her mind was playing tricks and he was bleeding. Realized too late what she'd heard.

Peter's geist crawled out from under Creach's body, half-spider and half-steam, extending spindly spoke-like legs that caught in the grass and pulled it farther into the open air. Magda squirmed away from it as hard as she could without rolling over on her own geist jar. On the ground, wreathed in red smoke, Creach began to convulse.

Liza and Winston lurched up—ready to help Creach or catch Magda, she wasn't sure—but as soon as they stepped into the red mist, the geist made a sound she hated being alive to hear, one part laugh and one part creaking coffin lid, and extended a dozen spider legs to mount their bodies like a climbing vine.

Creach sat up, coughed a lungful of red smoke. When he looked at Magda, she screamed. His eyes were no longer yellowy green, but lit from within by red points like embers, the same light she'd seen hovering in the middle of Peter's jar.

She pushed herself off the ground, staggering up to her feet though the motion hurt her head and made her want to throw up. Creach's face twisted, mouth and cheeks pulled back and eyes gaping, all the skin stretched tight like there was something in his head too large and urgent to contain. The light in his eyes was like looking into the heart of a star, small and distant but full of unstoppable energy.

Creach opened his mouth. Someone else spoke through it. A group of someones, shouting and wailing and screaming, garbled and full of terrible wrath. He began to heave his body up off the ground.

Magda whimpered. She wanted to run, but was trapped in her own indecision—staying in one place was surely fraught, but running could trigger explosive violence. Her limbs twitched with the effort of holding still. As she watched, Creach—the nightmare riding Creach—whipped his head around, looking for something, she knew not what.

"Boy," he hissed, in a voice not his own.

Peter huddled on the ground by the still, When he heard the voice, his eyes snapped up. Magda could see the whites. He was breathing hard through his mouth, panting. His body quivered.

"Dad?"

He shouldn't be around it, Magda thought, a memory of Peter's own words. The geist had ridden Peter's father until... what? What had Peter done, to take the geist from his father and to the Carnival?

Creach's body moved toward the still with a shuffling, bow-legged gait. Liza and Winston, limbs wreathed in red smoke, fell in behind him. Peter tried to stand, pressing a hand along the side of the still, but Creach's drink still had hold of him, and he fell. His hand left a dim smear on the bright copper skin.

"It's time to go home, boy," the geist hissed. "You took me from your father, and now I'm taking you."

Peter sat on the ground, blinking dumbly at the geist-ridden figures approaching. It was as if he'd expended all his coordination on getting Creach away from Magda.

The geist jar was in her hand, emitting a steady, certain buzz. She didn't remember taking it out. Three generations of nightmares caught in a bottle. Freeing herself from it was the only thing she wanted.

She couldn't think about this too long, or she wouldn't do it.

Magda squeezed the jar hard and wrestled the cork out of its neck.

For a moment, nothing. The dark opening at the jar's top beckoned. She tilted it for a better look.

The geist spurted from the jar, pouring itself out against the direction of gravity. It flowed up into the air, settled in a globous cloud in front of Magda, and seemed almost to sigh with relief. It was dark blue-black, pearlescent where it caught the light, like a dream of the bottom of the bog.

"Come on," Magda said, and the geist took her.

Water's weight crushing her. Kelp and weeds veining her hair, sliding between her fingers and toes. Her skin eroding, opening to the water and nibbling fish. Every nightmare she'd ever had of drowning and decomposition, swallowing her.

But this time there was no fear. She accepted the geist, stepped into it and let it wreathe through her hair and clothing. Breathed it deep into her lungs. Felt it settle inside of her as deep as her own womb. The geist was home, and she was home to it even as she dreamed of decay, like a wrecked skiff on the riverbed's bottom, still housing its dead captain.

Magda kept walking.

The geist-ridden distillers were closing on Peter. She got to them first and reached through the clouds of red smoke without fear, laying hands on their clothing and pulling them back. The geist surged, running down and out through her hands, and although she felt its departure as an arterial loss, she let it go.

The geist bled through the smoke shrouding Winston and Liza, forcing itself up and around their bodies, half-liquid, half-strangling snake. The smoke evaporated in its presence, Magda's geist engulfing and swallowing Peter's, leaving a ghostly mist with an uncertain purple hue behind. Liza and Winston collapsed.

Stationed in front of Peter, Creach reared up suddenly, spinning back as the geist inside him sensed the attack. He charged Magda, stumbling like a drunk, and Magda walked to meet him, catching his face in her hands and pressing it to hers in a touch that was almost tender. His skin felt clammy and thick in her fingers, and the geist offered her a memory of dead beavers half-decayed in the ruins of their dams, the fat in their flesh blossoming on the surface.

Everything in Creach was rotting.

"You wanted to own me," she said into Creach's vacant

eyes. She was half-herself, half-geist. "Here I am."

She opened her mouth and the geist poured into him.

She was with it enough to feel it ricochet inside of his body, saturating every vein and psychic pathway, bloating his memories and aspirations and schemes, wringing addictions out of him and sweeping every personal triumph and excess away. The geist took Creach out to sea, and with it the remnants of Peter's little geist.

She wondered if her geist had been like it long ago, a wisp of smoke. Three generations of growth and it was a power elemental.

She watched the last whiff of smoke inside of Creach's body vanish and felt full, like she'd had a pleasant meal.

The geist made a last, slow circuit of Creach's mind, looking for scraps, then retreated, flowing out of his mouth and eyes and ears and back up Magda's hands, flowing up her arms and into her, settling down in her viscera, seeping along her bones and tendons, making space for itself, coming home.

Because she had always been home.

"My dad," Peter told Magda, "had a terrible temper."

He was sobering up, still occasionally distracted by his own reflection in the copper. They sat beside each other, backs against the still.

Magda kicked her boots out in front of her. "That seems obvious."

"I shouldn't've done it. Enchanted him. But I was tired of him beating on me all the time. Thought I could help him."

Creach, or what had been Creach, sat in the yard's

center, blinking slowly at the lanterns going up in the stall across the street. He hadn't moved in hours.

Peter surveyed the man and nodded. "D'you think he'll come back to himself?"

"Dunno. Not until I'm well away from here, hopefully."

Magda touched the pockets on her dress, into which she'd tucked as many of Creach's special bottles as she could fit. She clinked when she moved.

"I'm real sorry, Peter. I did something terrible, bringing you to Creach. I thought it would be better for you, with him, than it woulda been for me. But I shouldn't've done it."

Peter blinked. "Yeah, but... You were getting rid of your geist, just like I wanted to do. You got rid of mine."

"It doesn't matter. I nearly left you with him."

"You didn't though."

Magda didn't know what to say. She had lost all good opinion of herself, and the forgiveness of the one she'd done harm to didn't alleviate the guilt.

"What's next for you, Magda? You gonna go home?"

"No," she said. "I think I have something else to do."

The bottles from Creach's store would fund her for weeks, months if she was clever. Long enough to get out of the bogs, go far out into the wider world.

She reached into a pocket in her dress, ran her thumb around the open mouth of the one empty bottle she carried.

The sun was setting over the bog, tinting the water copper. Lanterns were going up in the nearby booths and yards, but they wouldn't stay up for long. Almost time to leave. At full dark, the Carnival would end.

Creach's torso cast a long shadow across the yard. It nearly reached Magda's feet. Perhaps she would end up no better than him, hollowed out and silent in an empty lot somewhere.

Standing was work; the geist coursing through her had exhausted her body. She leaned against the still and looked out into the lane. Carnival patrons thronged the street as densely as before, oblivious to the spectral battle that had been fought not a hundred feet away. They moved with more urgency now as the carnival drew to a close. So many, just like Magda, trying to strike a bargain, to offload goods no one ever really wanted. She wondered where they had come from. She wondered their names.

Inside her gut, the geist whispered, *Hungry.*

ABOUT THE AUTHORS

AMANDA CASILE

Amanda is a speech pathologist and author living in New Jersey with her two daughters and husband. Her words have appeared in anthologies by Quill and Crow and Bag of Bones Press. When not writing or teaching kids to talk, she can often be found wandering the woods looking for ghosts.

Twitter: @BookishDuck
Instagram: @bookishduck_author

SARAH DAY

Sarah Day lives in the SF Bay Area with her cat and too many LED lights. She writes lots of different kinds of genre fiction, especially horror and scifi. She has been published in PseudoPod, Underland Arcana, The Future Fire, and other awesome places. Her debut novella, GREYHOWLER, will be released in the fall of 2023.

ROB FRANCIS

Rob Francis is an academic and writer based in Bedfordshire, England. He mainly writes short fantasy and horror, and his stories have appeared in magazines such as The Arcanist, Apparition Lit, Metaphorosis, Tales to Terrify and Weird Horror. Rob has also contributed stories to several anthologies, including DeadSteam and DeadSteam II by Grimmer & Grimmer books, Under the Full Moon's Light by Owl Hollow Press, and Alternative War by B Cubed Press. He is an affiliate member of the HWA. Rob lurks on Twitter @RAFurbaneco

KAY HANIFEN

Kay Hanifen was born on a Friday the 13th and once lived for three months in a haunted castle. So, obviously, she had to become a horror writer. Her articles have appeared in Ghouls Magazine, Screen Rant, The Borgen Project, and Leatherneck magazine; and her short stories have appeared in Strangely Funny VIII, Crunchy With Ketchup, Dark Shadows: The Gay Nineties, Wicked Newsletters, Fearful Fun, Death of a Bad Neighbor, Enchanted Entrapments, Diet Riot: A Fatterpunk Anthology, M is for Medical, Blood Moon, Terror in the Trenches, Slice of Paradise, Vinyl Cuts, Sherlock Holmes and Watson's Medical Mysteries, Beware the Bugs, Rockets and Robots, and Devil's Rejects. When she's not consuming pop culture with the voraciousness of a vampire at a 24-hour blood bank, you can usually find her with her two black cats or at kayhanifenauthor.wordpress.com.

DEREK HEATH

Derek Heath is a British horror author whose stories have so far been published in Wicked Shadow Press's Flash of the Dead and the second edition of Illustrated Worlds magazine. His first two novellas release at the beginning of April 2023 and with many more to come, he'll have to spend just about every second writing so that the demons don't catch up with him.

MACKENZIE HURLBERT

Mackenzie Hurlbert is a New England horror writer with publications in Coffin Bell, Not One of Us, Written Tales: Horror, The CT Literary Anthology, and Flash Fiction Magazine. She enjoys getting lost in the woods and is an avid collector of Pez dispensers and cool-looking rocks.

SELAH JANEL

Selah Janel is the author of titles that include The Inheritance and the Ruins of St. Louis. Her work has been included in The Dread Machine, Electric Spec, 34 Orchard, ParAbnormal, and others. An unrepentant theater geek, she has worked on many shows and events designing and building cosumes, including monsters for haunted events. She likes her music to rock, her vampires to use their fangs, her faeries to play mind games, and her princesses to hold their own.

DIXON MARCH

Dixon March is a reader and writer of weird fiction. At no point has she hosted a midnight radio talk show and/or intercepted dark messages from the stars. There are rumors she operates out of Omaha, Nebraska, US.

ELIN OLAUSSON

Elin Olausson is a fan of the weird and the unsettling. She is the author of the short story collection Growth and has had stories featured in The Ghastling, Luna Station Quarterly, Nightscript, and many other publications.

Elin's rural childhood made her love and fear the woods, and she firmly believes that a cat is your best companion in life. She lives in Sweden.

MARISCA PICHETTE

Marisca Pichette taps the blood of the world. More of her work appears in Strange Horizons, Vastarien, Fantasy Magazine, Flash Fiction Online, and PseudoPod, among others. Her speculative poetry collection, Rivers in Your Skin, Sirens in Your Hair, publishes from Android Press in April 2023. Find her on Twitter as @MariscaPichette and Instagram as @marisca_write.

MICHAEL QUAY

Michael Quay has been battling the stories that haunt him daily his entire life. He finally decided to let one out.

Twitter: @michaelqvay

BRYSON RICHARD

Bryson Richard lives in the Black Swamp region of Ohio.

Some of his stories have appeared in "What One Wouldn't Do", from Editor Scott J. Moses, "Step into the Light", from Bag of Bones Press, and "Mother: Tales of Love and Horror" from Weird Little Worlds.

Join our newsletter today and download a free book!
https://mailchi.mp/71e45b6d5880/welcomebook

More from Eerie River

Eerie River Publishing, is a small independant publishing house that is devoted to releasing quality dark fiction books and anthologies.

To stay up to date with all our new releases and upcoming giveaways, follow us on Facebook, Twitter, Instagram and YouTube. Sign up for our monthly newsletter and receive a free ebook Darkness Reclaimed, as our thank you gift.

https://mailchi.mp/71e45b6d5880/welcomebook

Interested in becoming a Patreon member?
Patreon membership gives you exclusive sneak peeks at upcoming books, early chapter releases, covers art as well as free ebooks and discounts on paperbacks.

https://www.patreon.com/EerieRiverPub.

IT CALLS FROM THE VEIL

EDITED BY LYNDSEY SMITH

EERIE RIVER PUBLISHING ANTHOLOGY

OF FIRE AND STARS
A DARK FANTASY LGBTQIA+ ANTHOLOGY
AVAILABLE EVERYWHERE